Once outside, Clark took off like a shot.

In a blur of seconds he was off his family's farm and charging down the road, promising himself that he wouldn't look back. *Damn wind is stinging my eyes*, he thought as he wiped at them with the back of his sleeve.

Clark reasoned that he could save time and, more important, money by running most of the way to Metropolis. It seemed like a logical place to go — it was the nearest big city, and he'd been there a few times on school trips so it wasn't completely strange to him. It might seem a little weird to see a kid just sprinting at high speed into the city, though, so he figured he'd run to the city limits and then catch a bus into town. That would attract less attention.

I'm going someplace where nobody knows that I'm different, where I can't cause any accidents, and where I can just be . . .

"Normal," Clark breathed, his own voice the only sound he could hear. "Just . . . normal."

SMALLVILLE™

Available from Little, Brown and Company

Runaway

SMALLVILLE ™

Runaway

Suzan Colón

Superman created by
Jerry Siegel and Joe Shuster

Hillsborough Community
College LRC

LITTLE, BROWN AND COMPANY
New York ⌀ An AOL Time Warner Company

For Mom and Dad; for my editors,
Steve Korté and Rich Thomas; for Amanda, David,
and Mike; and for both of them.

First Edition

The characters and events portrayed in this book are
fictitious. Any similarity to real persons, living or dead, is
coincidental and not intended by the author.

Library of Congress Cataloging-in-Publication Data

Colón, Suzan.
    Runaway / Suzan Colón. — 1st ed.
      p.   cm. — (Smallville ; #7)
    Sequel to: Buried secrets.
    Based on the WB television show "Smallville."
    Summary: When sixteen-year-old Clark Kent, later
known as Superman, runs away to Metropolis, he becomes
involved with Luna, a girl who calls herself a witch and
who lives with a group of runaways.
    ISBN 0-316-73476-4
    [1. Runaways — Fiction.   2. Heroes — Fiction.
3. Interpersonal relations — Fiction.   4. Witches —
Fiction.]   I. Title. II. Series.

PZ7.C71637Ru 2003
[Fic] — dc21   2003047444

10 9 8 7 6 5 4 3 2 1

Q-BF

Printed in the United States of America

Prologue

High above the brightly lit buildings of Metropolis, a quarter-moon shone like a lopsided smile. Underneath its watchful presence, a few miles away from the center of the city, a lone female figure sat on the rooftop of a dark, abandoned building.

The girl sat cross-legged in front of a white candle, shuffling a deck of cards. Slowly, she began to lay them down in a square pattern. An orange tabby kitten started walking on the cards, pushing them around with its paws.

"Hey, Rover, cut it out," the girl said, laughing. "I'm trying to read the future here, okay?" She scooped up the kitten and put it on her lap, where it curled up under her black fake-fur coat and purred loudly.

The girl went back to her cards. They weren't regular playing cards with hearts and spades; these cards had ornate drawings of swords, cups, towers, and medieval scenes. She brushed a lock of wavy blond hair out of her eyes and placed the last four cards in a straight row to the side of the others. She studied them intently.

The door to the roof squeaked open, and a boy stepped out and waved. "Hey," he called.

"Hey yourself, Skunk," the girl said with a grin.

"There's food downstairs," Skunk said. "Better hurry, though. The Tribe is way hungry tonight."

"The Tribe is way hungry every night. Is this one of your pizza specials?" she asked. Skunk nodded, and the girl wrinkled her nose. "Just save me a slice. I'll be down in a while."

"What's the good word from the cards?" Skunk asked. "Some money in our future, maybe? We could sure use it."

The girl scanned the cards again, a little frown of concentration creasing her brow. "Not just yet," she said. "But someone new is coming."

"Oh yeah? Someone cool?"

The frown left the girl's face as she lifted one card out of the spread. The Page of Swords. It pictured a young man with broad shoulders and dark hair holding a sword — the symbol for the element of air. The card represented someone who was hopeful, adventurous, and wanted to help people in trouble. A hero.

That was the card's general meaning. Now she needed more information.

Her focus grew soft, and the card became almost hazy in her gaze until, after a second or two, she no longer even saw it. Instead, she saw a form taking shape: a guy of about her own age — sixteen — tall, with dark hair. She couldn't make out his features but she could tell what he was like, almost as though she could look right into his heart. A warm feeling spread over her. And there was something else that she couldn't quite make out. . . . He was different somehow. Special.

Slowly, the vision faded away. The girl looked over her shoulder at Skunk.

"Someone very cool," she said with a smile.

Chapter 1

"Clark, you're going to miss the school bus!" Martha Kent called up to her son.

"'Morning, Mom," Clark Kent said as he trotted down the stairs to the kitchen. "Don't worry about the bus. If I miss it, I'll just run to school." He smiled at her as he opened the fridge and rooted around for some breakfast.

"Clark, just because you can run to school at sixty miles an hour doesn't mean you shouldn't make an appearance on the bus every now and then." Martha threw a knowing look at Clark. She was always worried that someone might find out about his "special abilities," as she called them. But she didn't say any more about it; she seemed a little distracted as she hurried around the kitchen.

"Speaking of being late," Clark teased as he tried to get the old toaster to heat some frozen waffles, "shouldn't you be at the Luthor mansion by now?" Clark's mother was the assistant to Lionel Luthor, one of the richest men in the country and the father of Clark's friend Lex Luthor.

"As a matter of fact, I should," said Martha. "But I forgot that the mortgage payment is due at the bank this morning, and your father went to the Dixons' farm to help him out while his tractor is being repaired. He could be gone all day." She sighed. "That payment can't be late, so I guess *I'm* going to have to be."

"I have an idea," Clark said, giving up on the toaster and warming up the waffles with his heat vision. "Why don't I stop by Mr. Dixon's and give the mortgage check to Dad? Then he can take it to the bank and you won't be late."

"What about you?" Martha asked. "Don't you have a big chemistry test this morning?"

Clark nodded, chewing. "Mmm-hmm. But I can just run over to Mr. Dixon's, give Dad the payment, and run to school."

"Are you sure, sweetie? I really don't want you to be late. . . ."

"Absolutely," Clark said, giving her a syrup-laced kiss on the cheek. "Don't worry about a thing, Mom."

❧ ❧ ❧ ❧

Clark felt good as he tore down the road that led from the Kent Farm to the Dixons'. The autumn air felt cool on his face as he became a blur of speed, everything around him looking like it was in slow motion. He'd been studying hard for this chemistry test, and he felt really prepared. And he was happy for the chance to make things a little easier for his mom, who was having a hard time balancing home life with her job.

Clark left the short grasses of his family's dairy farm behind and was soon surrounded on either side of the road by the tall cornfields of the Dixons' farm. He just had a few miles to go before reaching the main house, where he'd probably find his father.

The wind roared in Clark's ears as he ran. He thought about the upcoming Halloween dance — he knew that Lana Lang, the girl he'd had a crush on forever, was going as Scarlett O'Hara, but Clark wasn't sure what he'd dress up as. Going as Rhett Butler would probably be way too obvious . . .

Lost in thought and traveling fast, Clark didn't see or hear his father's tractor emerging from the cornfield right ahead of him until it was too late.

CHAPTER 2

Dad!" Clark cried. "Dad, are you okay?!"

At first, the shock of impact made Clark think he'd somehow run into a tree, even though he knew there weren't any trees in the middle of the cornfield. But a second later, when he got up from the dirt road, he was horrified to see that he'd collided with the tractor. The front end of it was now smashed like an accordion, and lying on the ground a dozen feet away was Clark's father.

"Dad," Clark pleaded as he knelt next to Jonathan Kent's limp body, "Dad, please wake up . . ." Trying not to panic, Clark focused his eyes intently to scan his father with his X-ray vision, another of the abilities he'd recently discovered he had. No head injuries — *Thank God,*

Clark thought — but he saw that Jonathan's collarbone was broken, making his shoulder twist at an odd angle.

"Clark . . . ," Jonathan moaned. "Son, are you all right?" It was just like his father, Clark thought, to be hurt himself but worrying about a kid who couldn't be affected by bullets, tractor crashes, or almost anything else.

"I'm fine," Clark said, trying not to appear as frightened as he felt, "but I've got to get you to a hospital."

ை ை ை ை

"Clark!" Martha Kent called, running down the hospital hallway. "Where's your father? Is he all right?"

Clark nodded nervously. It had been horrible having to call his mother to tell her to meet him at the hospital.

Just then, the doctor beckoned them into a room where Jonathan lay on a bed, his arm in a sling, his face badly bruised.

"Hi honey," Jonathan said, his voice sounding woozy. "Don't worry, I'm fine."

Martha looked from her husband to the doctor for confirmation. "He is if 'fine' means having a broken collarbone, a dislocated shoulder, and a herniated disc in his lower back," the doctor said. "I'd say you're *going* to be fine, but only after a week or so of bed rest. It could have been much worse, though. How did you say this happened, Mr. Kent?"

"I . . . I hit something," Jonathan said hesitantly. A wave of guilt washed over Clark, and he lowered his head. Martha looked from her husband to her son, sensing there was more to the story than they could reveal at the moment.

The doctor frowned. "Well, I'll be back in a little while to check on you. If you're doing okay, we can let you go home tonight."

As soon as the doctor left, Clark explained what happened to his mother. "I'm sorry, Dad," he said. "I was going too fast, and I didn't see you coming. . . ."

"It's not your fault, son," Jonathan said, pained

more by the sorrowful look on Clark's face than by his injuries. "I remembered the mortgage payment and decided to come back early. Quit worrying," he said, reaching out with his good arm to pat Clark's hand. "I'm okay. Get to school and I'll see you at dinner."

Reluctantly, Clark left, but only after Martha pushed him out the door.

❦ ❦ ❦ ❦

It was almost lunch period by the time Clark got to school, and the first person he saw in the hallway was Terrance Reynolds, the principal of Smallville High School. He'd only been there a short time before the students started calling him Terrance "The Terror" Reynolds behind his back. Unfortunately, he saw Clark, too.

"Clark Kent!" he called sternly. He motioned for Clark to follow him, and they walked wordlessly down the hall to his office.

"You're late, Mr. Kent," the principal said, closing the door behind them. "Again."

"Mr. Reynolds, I can explain —"

"That chemistry exam is a very important part of your grade, but I can see by your lateness that this isn't of much importance to you."

"Mr. Reynolds —" Clark tried to interrupt, but the principal held up his hand.

"I'm not interested in excuses, Mr. Kent. You've had too many of them in the past, and frankly, they're not very creative." The principal sat behind his desk and regarded Clark with his usual harsh expression. "It's my opinion that the only way to get you to take your studies seriously and live up to your potential is by imposing serious punishment when it's needed. So I'm giving you detention for the next month. And not another word, unless you want more."

"But — !" Clark's eyes grew wide. Was this really happening? Since Mr. Reynolds had become the new principal at Smallville High, he'd had it in for Clark. It had been that way from the moment he'd found out that Clark was friends with Lex, who had been Mr. Reynolds's least favorite student at Excelsior Prep. He'd been the principal at the exclusive private school until he tried to expel Lex, and Lionel Luthor had him fired for it. But surely Mr. Reynolds would listen to reason once he found out what had happened to Clark's father.

The only problem was getting a word in, and it didn't look like that was going to happen. "All right, Mr. Kent, no extracurricular activities, either. And that includes the Halloween dance next week."

"Mr. Reynolds, I —" Clark tried again, but it was no use.

"And," said the principal, delivering the final blow, "an F in chemistry for this semester. I suggest you leave now, Mr. Kent, unless you want to try for expulsion as well. Dismissed."

Great, Clark thought as he glumly walked out of Mr. Reynolds's office. *What else can go wrong?*

CHAPTER 3

The rest of the afternoon was a different kind of blur than when Clark was running super fast. Now it felt like the world was moving normally, and he was the one stuck in slow motion.

He wished his best friend, Pete Ross, wasn't out of town with his family. Pete's aunt had gotten sick, and he and his parents had gone to Grandville to help her out for a week until she got better. Pete and Clark had been best friends since they were little, and Pete was the only person outside of Clark's family who knew about Clark's secret, about his abilities, about what was hidden in the Kents' storm cellar.

Clark sighed, wanting to unload about the day to someone who would understand. Lex would be busy at work; he was older than Clark and the heir to a multibillion-dollar corporation, so he probably didn't have time for this kind of stuff. Chloe Sullivan was another close friend, but she and Clark had recently gone through an awkward near-dating situation that had left things a little strained between them.

That left Lana Lang. Clark's mood lifted a little as he headed for the Talon, the coffeehouse where Lana worked as a manager.

Clark and Lana had a strong friendship, even though it was pretty complicated. He had a fierce crush on her that had never come to anything because, at first, Lana had been with a longtime boyfriend, Whitney Fordman. By the time Whitney had joined the Marines and Lana decided she couldn't cope with a long-distance relationship, she and Clark had developed such a deep friendship that they weren't able to take it to the next level.

Part of the problem was obvious: Lana had told Clark in the past that she always felt he was holding something back from her. And she was right. Clark knew he would never be able to reveal himself to her completely. Yet their friendship was still so strong that they'd managed to overcome even this obstacle, and Lana was one of Clark's closest friends. Just by listening, Lana would be able to take some of the nastiness away from this day.

❧ ❧ ❧ ❧

The Talon was busy, as it was most afternoons. It was a labor of love for Lana, who had transformed it — with Lex's help — from a condemned building into a popular hangout. It was Lana's hope that it would one day be restored to its former glory as a movie theater so it would be just the way it had been when her parents met there years ago. They had died in the meteor shower that hit Smallville when Lana was little, and she was determined to preserve their memory any way she could.

"Hey," Clark said, sitting at the counter.

Lana turned from filling the cappuccino machine. "Hey Clark. What's up?"

"Well, I've had what you could call an interesting day." He sighed. "I could really use a friend."

He looked at her hopefully, even though he had no doubt that Lana would be there for him as she always had. So he was totally unprepared for what she said next.

"Then . . . maybe you should talk to Lex."

Clark wasn't sure he'd heard her right. "What — Lana, is something wrong?"

Lana put down the coffee filter. "Look, Clark," she began. "I know it seems like I'm bringing this up out of the blue, but I've been thinking a lot about us — about our friendship, our relationship, whatever you want to call it." She tried to smile to lighten the heaviness of what she was saying, but it didn't work. "See, that's just the problem. I don't know *what* we are. I used to think we were friends, but then there was that time when you told me you had . . . well, that you had feelings for me." Lana was interrupted by a flash of memory: Clark coming into the Talon, admitting that he liked her as more than a friend, and kissing her passionately. She was surprised at how fresh it was in her mind, and how it could still throw her off balance. She tried to get her thoughts back in order.

"Then," Lana continued, "you said you just wanted to be friends again. But you can't do a one-eighty like that and expect everything to go back to the way it was."

Lana took a second to catch her breath. It was only a week ago that Chloe had bluntly asked her if she was avoiding Clark. Lana herself hadn't realized it until Chloe pointed out that Lana had been going out of her way not to come along whenever someone in their tight-knit group suggested going to a movie or to one of the school football games. "I don't think you're mad at Pete," Chloe had said, "so it's either me or Clark. Fess up."

It wasn't about Chloe. After Lana thought about it, she realized that she felt so confused by her feelings for Clark, and by his feelings for her, that she'd unconsciously begun to avoid him.

Chloe had urged her to talk to Clark about it. "You can't run away from your feelings, whatever they are," she'd said. "And neither can he. This discussion is long overdue between you two, and maybe if you get it out in the open, Clark will be honest with you, once and for all."

That was what Lana had been hoping for — that Clark would tell her how he really, truly felt about her. She needed to know whether he saw her as a friend or as something more. There were so many times that she'd gotten used to being one or the other, and then he'd send a signal that confused her completely. Maybe if she forced the issue he would finally open up about why he was so secretive, why he would only let her get so close before he pushed her away.

But now that her feelings were out in the open, it didn't look like Clark was going to say anything at all. He was just sitting there, looking utterly shocked and stung. Lana had known that this talk might be painful for both of them, but she had promised herself she would say what she needed to, no matter what.

"Clark, what I'm trying to say is . . . I'm just not sure I can be your friend right now. I think I need to take some time to figure out what we are to each other. And I think you need to do the same."

Almost as soon as the words left her mouth,

Lana wished she could take them back. Clark looked far more wounded than she'd expected him to. She could practically feel his sadness.

"All right," he said softly. "If that's how you feel." He stood up and walked quickly toward the door.

"Clark, wait —"

"Miss?" came a voice from one of the tables. "Can we get some more coffee over here?"

CHAPTER 4

Martha Kent dished out salad as she watched her husband and son sitting silently at the dinner table. Even though they were not related by blood, at this moment the two were more alike than they realized. As they sat there, each had the same grave expression as he stared into space. Clark would look at his father mournfully, then look away. A second later Jonathan would look over at Clark, start to say something, and stop himself.

Martha broke the silence. "Clark, don't worry about that F in chemistry. Your father is going to call Mr. Reynolds tomorrow and tell him what happened. He'll understand, and you'll just take a make-up test."

"I know," Clark said in a quiet voice.

Martha sat down and put her hand on Clark's shoulder. "Sweetie, did something else happen today? Anything you want to talk about?" Clark just shook his head.

Jonathan raised his eyebrows at Martha, who shrugged helplessly. "I'm going to be fine, son," Jonathan offered cheerily. "Really. I'll be as good as new in no time."

Clark looked up at his father, then down at his plate. It was full of macaroni and cheese that his mother had made. She'd said that after a day like this, they needed some comfort food. This was one of Clark's favorites, and normally it would have thrilled him to pieces. But tonight he couldn't eat a bite of it.

To fill the silence, Martha chatted about work — something about LuthorCorp building a new chemical plant in Metropolis and the problems going on with the project. Clark tried to listen, but when his father winced in pain after reaching for the saltshaker, he just went back to feeling incredibly guilty.

When dinner was finally over, Clark retreated to the barn.

❧ ❧ ❧ ❧

Thousands of stars sparkled brightly over Smallville, but Clark saw none of them as he stared absently through the barn doors. He was up in the hayloft, part of which his father had set aside for him to have a little extra space; there, Clark had a desk, his stereo, his books, and some privacy. It was a good place to think.

Normally, he would have been looking at the stars through his telescope, doing his homework, or hanging out with Lana, who sometimes rode her horse over to the Kent farm. But tonight, Clark sat on the couch trying to figure out whether this had been the worst day of his life or just one of the top five.

Let's see, he thought, *I started the day by hurting my Dad and totaling the tractor. I was late for a test that I could have taken and passed in about a minute, but instead I got an F for the semester. And then —*

Clark stopped. Perhaps the harshest of the day's events had been what happened at the Talon.

Why today, Lana? Clark wondered. *Of all days, why did you have to tell me today that you don't want to be friends?*

It was hard to imagine life without Lana in it. Sure, he still had Pete, Lex, and Chloe, but Lana was different. Clark's feelings for her ran deeper than they did for practically anybody he could think of. They could say things to each other that they couldn't say to anyone else.

Well, almost, Clark thought. There were things he would never be able to tell Lana. And there were things he *had* told Lana that he never should have.

Clark wished for the thousandth time there was some way he could erase that whole episode from his mind. Instead, it began playing out before him again.

It had all started innocently enough, when Clark bought a Smallville High School class ring. His father had told him that they couldn't afford it, but Clark had taken all the allowance money he'd saved to buy the ring, which was gold and set with a ruby. Only it hadn't been a ruby at all — the stone was actually a red meteorite.

Meteorites were common around Smallville since they'd rained destruction on the town fourteen years ago. The meteor shower killed Lana's parents, made Lex become bald . . . *And brought me here*, Clark thought. The knowledge that he'd been part of such a terrible disaster weighed on him heavily.

The green meteorites were not only a painful reminder of those things, but they also had a deadly effect on Clark. Whenever he came near them, his strength, speed, and all other abilities disappeared, and the agony they brought on was unbearable. He felt the life was being slowly, horribly sucked out of him.

The red meteorites, though, had a totally different effect.

Clark still remembered the rush he got when he slipped the class ring on his finger. Suddenly, he'd felt more confident, more alive than ever before. But that great feeling had quickly morphed into something dangerous, and in only a matter of days he was out of control, using his powers in front of people and hurting others.

But before things had gotten completely out of hand, there was the afternoon when he calmly walked into the Talon and told Lana what he'd been wanting to say for ages. Then (and he still couldn't believe he'd done this), he kissed her deeply, in a way that let Lana know he wanted to be *much* more than friends.

After that, things went very, very wrong. Clark had borrowed Lex's Ferrari to take Lana out later that night, only to blow it with her completely by hitting on another girl. And then —

Enough, Clark winced, halting the memory. That definitely hadn't been one of his better days. But was it as bad as this one?

He tried to think of something that would jog him out of this mood, and he smiled as a childhood memory came to him: When he was little and had a bad day, his mother would sit him down at the kitchen table with a big plate of peanut butter-chip cookies, Clark's favorite, and a glass of milk. "These," she'd say, ruffling his dark hair, "are magic cookies. And if you eat a few, you'll forget whatever is bothering you." Then she'd wink at him and watch as he happily devoured them.

Hey, if it worked then, maybe it'll work now. Clark turned the lights off in the barn and headed back to the house.

☙ ☙ ☙ ☙

From outside, Clark could see his parents framed by the open kitchen window, his father at the table with his arm in the sling, his mother by his side. He was about to go in when he heard his mother say, "Jonathan, please, stop looking at those bills . . ."

Something in her voice made Clark hesitate. It wasn't anger, more like pleading. He didn't want to eavesdrop, but sometimes his parents told him things were okay when they weren't, to keep from worrying him, and he wanted to know what was going on.

As Clark stepped to the side of the door so his parents wouldn't see him, he heard his father sigh with exasperation. "Martha, I can't stop looking at them, or thinking about them."

"Jonathan, you've had a big day," Martha said. "You should be resting —"

"I can't afford to rest," Jonathan insisted. "The bills were already pretty bad, but now we need a new tractor — that's going to cost thousands . . ."

"I know, but we'll manage somehow," Martha soothed. "We've had problems before, and we've always found a way to get through them."

Clark held his breath. The guilt he felt for adding to his parents' money worries with the wrecked tractor made him want to run back to the barn. But he stayed and listened when his father said, "Martha . . . there's something else."

His mother was quiet for a moment. "I know what you're going to say, and — and, well, we'll figure that out too! I mean, we've been putting a little money aside here and there —"

"You know it's not nearly enough for tuition, books, all the other expenses. I'd been counting on his good grades getting him a scholarship, but after this F today —"

"Jonathan, you know that won't stick when

we tell them what happened . . ." But Martha's voice trailed off.

"I know, but even still . . . Martha, I just don't know how we can afford to send Clark to college."

Clark felt a pain unlike anything the meteorites had ever done to him. *All their worrying . . . all these problems*, he thought. *It's all because of me.*

He couldn't bear to hear any more. As quietly as he could, he crept around the house and went in through the front door, up the stairs, and into his room.

He knew what he had to do.

CHAPTER 5

It will be better for them this way, Clark thought.

In the darkness of his room, Clark moved as quickly but as quietly as he could. He reached up to the top shelf of his closet and pulled out a large knapsack, bigger than the backpack he carried to school each day. He stuffed in a few pairs of jeans and some flannel shirts; then he went to his bureau and got out sweaters, T-shirts, socks, and underwear. Those too went in the knapsack.

What else? He didn't know what he would need besides clothes, so he went around the room grabbing random things — some of his favorite CDs and his Discman. A book he was reading for English class, *The Catcher in the Rye.* He went to his desk — pens? notebook? his old baseball cards?

Clark stopped and took a deep breath. *Okay, I've got to chill*. He realized he was freaking out and trying to stuff as much of home into one knapsack as he could.

One thing on his desk caught his eye — a framed photo of himself with his parents when he was about six. It was taken on the day his father had put up a tire swing in the backyard, and the three of them were smiling. A happy family.

A wave of emotion threatened to interrupt Clark's plan, and he hastily shoved the photo deep into the bag.

Clark then reached into the back of a drawer in his desk and pulled out a box where he kept stuff that was important to him. There were things that he'd collected as a kid: coins, fishing lures from trips with his father, a bear claw he'd found in the forest. There were newspaper articles that he'd started clipping a few years ago. Some were about the meteor storm that had hit Smallville, others were stories from all around the world about kids with special abilities — one who could lift a car, another who could walk on burning coals. For a while, Clark had looked for stories like this in the hopes of finding others like himself. He stopped when he found out that they were hoaxes.

Clark pushed all of it aside and found a small wad of folded money. He quickly counted it: $350, his allowance money that had been refunded from the class ring company after Chloe revealed that they'd used meteorites instead of real rubies in the rings. Clark didn't know if that was enough cash or too little for what he was about to do.

There was just one thing left. Tearing a page from his notebook, he hastily scribbled a note.

He was almost finished when he heard his parents' footsteps as they came up the stairs. Clark froze; he didn't want them to notice that he was still awake and possibly come in to say good night. Luckily he hadn't turned the light on when he'd come into his room. A moment later, though, he heard his parents shut the door to their bedroom.

Placing the note on his pillow and pulling on his coat, Clark took one last look around his room. Then he slowly slipped down the stairs and into the night.

❦ ❦ ❦ ❦

Once outside, Clark took off like a shot.

In a blur of seconds he was off his family's farm and charging down the road, promising himself that he wouldn't look back. *Damn wind is stinging my eyes*, he thought as he wiped at them with the back of his sleeve.

Clark reasoned that he could save time and, more important, money by running most of the way to Metropolis. It seemed like a logical place to go — it was the nearest big city, and he'd been there a few times on school trips, so it wasn't completely strange to him. It might seem a little weird for a kid to be seen sprinting at high speed into the city, though, so he figured he'd run to the city limits and then catch a bus into town. That would attract less attention.

He hadn't actually gone that far when, without realizing why, Clark found himself slowing down. He took a moment to catch his breath and look around. There were no signs or landmarks, nothing but the road and acres of corn on either side. But then Clark realized where he was.

This is where they found me, he thought, *the day of the meteor shower.*

Clark had always known he was adopted, but he'd never really given much thought to it beyond wondering who his birth parents were. Because he loved Jonathan and Martha Kent as his own parents, the question of *how* they had come to adopt Clark had never really entered his mind.

Not until the day, about a year ago, his father had shown him what was hidden in the storm cellar.

A soft breeze rustled the stalks as it wove through the cornfield, the tall plants flashing dark green under the moonlight. The crater that had been burned into this spot was gone, planted over long ago. But Clark's parents had told him the real story of how they'd found him so vividly that he could almost see it now.

The Kents had been driving from town on the same road where Clark was standing. His mother had told him what looked like fire began raining from the sky, and there were explosions all around them. Clark's father had just managed to swerve their truck out of the way of a meteorite that tore up the road in front of them on impact. But as he swiveled out of the way, they ran off the road and rolled into the cornfield.

They were suspended upside down, each checking to see if the other was all right. Then Jonathan and Martha looked outside the smashed windows of the truck and saw a little boy grinning at them. He was standing barefoot on ground that was still smoking from the heat of the meteorite. And behind him . . .

Clark thought back to the day in the cellar when his father had pulled the canvas tarp off the spaceship, remembering the shock that had gone through him when Jonathan said, "This is how you came into our world, son. The day of the meteor shower." From that day forward, whenever Clark thought about his adoption or his birth parents, the question in his mind had changed from *who am I?* to *what am I?*

That's over now, he thought. *I'm going someplace*

where nobody knows that I'm different, where I can't cause any accidents, and where I can just be . . .

"Normal," Clark breathed, his own voice the only sound he could hear. "Just . . . normal."

He started running again.

CHAPTER 6

Metropolis! Last stop!"

The bus driver's shout woke Clark with a start, and it took him a second to remember the rest of last night. He'd found the bus stop on the outskirts of the city, and, sometime in the early morning hours, the bus had come. After running all night, Clark had fallen asleep almost as soon as he sat down.

Now, he groggily hitched his knapsack up on his shoulder and filed out of the bus with the other passengers and into confusion.

All around him in the brightly lit bus station, hundreds of people were rushing in different directions. Everyone seemed to have somewhere to go and was in a major hurry to get there. He watched with envy as the other people from the bus were found by their friends or families and hugged warmly, then taken home.

It was hitting him now — he was really alone, away from everyone and everything he knew for the first time in his life. Clark stood by the bus for a moment, looking around, trying to figure out what to do next.

"There you are!" he heard someone say. Clark saw a pretty girl about his age coming toward him, wavy blond hair flowing behind her and a big smile spreading across her face. The person she was looking for must have been behind him.

But no, the girl went right up to Clark, threw her arms open and drew him close in a warm hug. "It's been so long I bet you hardly recognized me," she said.

"Um, I think you might have me mistaken —"

The girl drew her face up to Clark's ear. "Three dudes are scoping you out to steal your stuff," she whispered. "Play along until we're outside. Trust me."

Clark wasn't afraid — unless the guys were armed with meteorites, they were no threat to him. But he wasn't anxious to attract attention, and fighting off attempted muggers within his first five minutes in Metropolis wasn't exactly the way he wanted to start his day.

"You're right!" he said brightly, returning the girl's hug. "It's like I hardly know you."

"C'mon," she said, taking him by the arm. "The others are waiting for us." She said that part loud enough to be heard as she led Clark toward the exit. Clark looked behind him as they walked away. Sure enough, three sketchy-looking men were watching them leave, looking like snakes who just saw a bird that they'd been lining up for lunch fly away.

"Sorry if I took you by surprise," the girl said as they headed out of the bus station. "But I've seen those guys in action, and they're pretty fierce. And not in a good way. They figure kids who are just off the bus are easy targets."

"Wow," Clark said, suddenly feeling very naive. "Thanks for looking out for me."

"My name's Luna," the girl said, sticking her hand out.

Clark took her hand and shook his head slightly. "I'm sorry — did you say your name was *Lana*?"

The girl laughed. "No, *Luna*. Well, it's actually LuAnne, but I like Luna better. It's the name of a moon goddess. It also means 'crazy,' but don't let that scare you."

Luna had a warm, open smile, and Clark liked her immediately. "I'm Clark Kent," he said.

"Clark, huh? I've never met anyone named Clark before," Luna said.

"It's my mother's maiden name," he replied. "It doesn't have any other meaning. Except maybe 'confused' and 'starving.'"

Luna laughed. "Then I think you'd better come with me so you don't get ripped off by some waiter."

❧ ❧ ❧ ❧

Martha Kent checked her watch. She didn't have much time to make breakfast for Clark and Jonathan before she had to run to work, but she knew if she didn't her son and injured husband would probably eat cold macaroni and cheese washed down with milk drunk straight from the bottle. She smiled to herself as she began to scramble some eggs, hoping she wouldn't be too late and that today would be better than yesterday.

"Hey, what's this?" Jonathan Kent walked slowly into the kitchen and kissed his wife on the cheek. "A businesswoman like you has no time for cooking."

"I didn't think you'd be up to flipping omelets with that arm." She helped Jonathan into a chair; she could tell from his stiff movements that he was still in pain. "How are you feeling?"

"I'm fine," he said. "It's not so bad. I've got too much to do to lie around the house, anyway."

"Jonathan Kent, don't you dare. Clark can take care of the farm work when he gets home from school. Speaking of which . . . Clark!" she called. "Breakfast!"

Martha waited to hear her son's familiar "Be right down, Mom," but there was nothing. Maybe he was still in the shower? She didn't hear any water running . . .

"Have you seen Clark this morning?" she asked. Jonathan shook his head, also thinking it strange that their son wasn't downstairs yet.

It was unusual for Clark to oversleep, Martha thought as she walked up the stairs. She paused in front of Clark's door and knocked softly. "Clark? Sweetie, are you up?" Hearing nothing, she slowly opened the door.

Clark's room was usually a little cluttered, as any sixteen-year-old boy's room would be. But this morning it looked like it had been ransacked. The closet door was open, all the hangers pushed to one side; the drawers of Clark's bureau and desk had also been left open. Only the bed was perfectly made as though it hadn't been slept in, and there was a note resting on the pillow.

DEAR MOM AND DAD,
    PLEASE DON'T FREAK OUT. I'M GOING
AWAY FOR A WHILE TO MAKE SOME MONEY
SO I WON'T BE SUCH A HUGE BURDEN ON

YOU. YOU KNOW I'LL BE OKAY, SO DON'T
WORRY! I'LL TRY NOT TO BE GONE TOO
LONG.
    I LOVE YOU BOTH SO MUCH.
    CLARK

"Jonathan!" Martha cried in anguish.

CHAPTER 7

While Luna studied the menu at the fast-food restaurant they'd gone to, Clark studied her. She was really pretty, in a wild-looking way — she was nothing like Lana, Chloe, or any of the other girls he knew in Smallville. Her dirty-blond hair was a mass of waves. She wore black eyeliner, but the rest of her angelic face was free of makeup; the effect was kind of innocent, kind of not. She was wearing a long black coat that looked like it was made out of teddy bear fur, a white T-shirt, pink bell-bottom cords, and black Converse sneakers. She looked like a fugitive from a band or something.

"Hmmm," she mused. "What can I get for a buck and ten cents . . ."

Clark reached into his knapsack. "I've got money —"

"*Shhhh!*" Luna admonished him. "That's not the kind of thing you want to say too loud in this neighborhood, if you want to hang on to what money you've got."

He leaned in close to her and spoke quietly. "Get whatever you want," he said. "It's on me."

"Is your last name Luthor?" Luna asked, eyebrows raised.

Clark grinned at the irony. "No, but I've got enough to get us a decent breakfast. And besides, it's the least I can do after you kept me out of trouble."

❧ ❧ ❧ ❧

Clark thought he was hungry, but Luna ate like she hadn't seen food in days. Two huge hamburgers, her own large bag of fries, some of his fries, and a giant strawberry shake disappeared into her small frame. Finally, she leaned back, sated. "Whew," she sighed. "Thanks, Clark. So do you actually have any place to stay here in Metropolis?"

"Not really," Clark admitted, wondering what exactly he'd thought he was going to do once he got here.

"You must've bugged out of home pretty quick," Luna said. "What did your parents do to you?"

"Nothing," Clark said, surprised. "My parents are great — they never did anything bad to me, nothing that would make me want to leave."

Luna was confused. "Then why'd you run away?"

Clark frowned, trying to find a way to answer, but before he could, Luna leaned forward and gently took his hand. "I know how it is," she said. "You think you're all alone, that nobody else could possibly relate to what you've got going on. You feel like you've got this big bad secret, and not a soul in the world would understand."

"Yeah," Clark said, surprised at how much Luna was describing what he felt, though there was no way she could know just how big a secret he had.

She nodded. "I felt like that too, once."

"And then what happened?"

"Someone rescued me at the bus station," she smiled. "Maybe you'd better come home with me. Metropolis can be kind of scary if you don't know where you're going, or who to trust."

"Well —" Clark hesitated, but there didn't seem to be too many options. He smiled at Luna. "How do I know I can trust you?"

"A long time ago, in a past life, I was a Girl Scout. I know, I know, I don't exactly look like one, but it's true," she said as Clark laughed along with her. "And there's only one thing I can do that will let you know that you can absolutely, positively, without a doubt trust me."

Clark watched as Luna lifted two fingers up to her forehead in a salute. "Scout's honor," she said. They both erupted in laughter.

֍ ֍ ֍ ֍

"Yes, Mrs. Kent, I'll definitely call if I hear from him. Don't worry — I'm sure he's fine." Lex hung up the phone as his father strode purposefully into the room.

"Was that Martha Kent?" Lionel said, without a greeting to Lex. "Where is she? She's late."

"I'm afraid you don't have an assistant today," Lex said. "Mrs. Kent has a family emergency. Apparently, Clark ran away from home last night."

Lionel's eyebrows rose in surprise. "Really," he said. "That seems unlike him. I never pictured Clark Kent as having a rebellious streak." Lionel sat down on the big leather couch in Lex's office. "I've learned that people who seem uncomplicated are far more . . . interesting than we give them credit for."

Lex didn't respond. When his father had gone temporarily blind after an accident and had come to live with Lex in the Luthor Mansion in Smallville, Lionel had become curious about Clark, about the Kents, about the strange things that sometimes happened around the town. Lex didn't want to encourage his father's interest, partly out of protective feelings for Clark, and partly because Lex had his own questions about his friend.

Even the way they'd met had been incredibly strange. Lex remembered driving along a road (too fast, as usual) and his tire blowing out. He lost control of his car, and he could do nothing but watch in horror as he crashed right into a kid and then flew off a bridge. He'd lost consciousness after that.

When he came to, Lex found that he was unhurt, and so was the boy he'd hit. Not only that, but the kid — Clark Kent — had saved Lex from drowning by pulling him out of the submerged car. Clark insisted later that he'd stepped out of the way in time. But the way Lex remembered it, he knew he'd crashed into him full force.

Later, when the car was dragged from the river, no one was able to explain why the roof looked like it had been peeled back like tinfoil. The questions of how Clark had survived and how he had saved him nagged at Lex almost constantly.

But he tried to push them aside because Clark had become his first friend in Smallville — perhaps his first true friend ever. He didn't suck up to Lex because he was rich, and he didn't hold it against Lex that the Luthors were generally mistrusted and disliked for owning most of the businesses in town.

No, Clark just seemed to like Lex, to look up to him as an older brother. And Lex, whose mother was dead and whose father was cold and occasionally dangerous, liked that feeling.

And yet . . .

"Something troubling you, son?" Lionel asked.

"I was just thinking about our development plans for lower Metropolis," Lex lied, wondering where Clark could have gone, and why. "There's a chance that those old buildings may qualify as historical landmarks. If they do, we'll have to find another location for the new chemical plant."

Lionel laughed. "The Luthors make history, Lex, we don't preserve it. Don't you worry. A bunch of old buildings won't stand in the way of progress."

His father's voice was light, but there was something in it that made Lex wonder what he was up to.

CHAPTER 8

Clark had never been on the subway before, and this first time made him feel like he was in another world. It was incredibly noisy and busy and the train car was packed with people, even in the middle of the day. He and Luna were smushed together in a way that might have embarrassed him a little if it were anyone else, but there was something about her that made him feel unusually relaxed. She was like an instant best friend.

It would have been obvious to anyone who bothered to notice that Clark wasn't from around here, the way he was looking around at everything and everybody. There was so much wide, open space in Smallville that you could go for miles and not see a soul; here, it seemed like everywhere you went people were packed together, always in a rush. It was amazing.

Luna tugged on his sleeve to get his attention. "This is our stop," she said, leading him out onto the platform.

When they got out to the street, Clark thought Luna must have made a mistake. They were surrounded by dark, old-looking buildings that had either fallen down or looked like they were about to. Some of them were boarded up completely, and there were no stores, markets, coffee bars, or anything that would show that the neighborhood was alive.

They walked for a few blocks before stopping in front of a five-story building that, a long time ago, had been a stately, beautiful townhouse. It had a heavy, wooden front door with stained glass windows set in the top. A few of the panes were broken, leaving only fragments of red and blue glass. There were carved stone ledges by each window, ornate but crumbling. The building had probably been amazing in its day, just like the other ones around it. But right at the moment none of them looked like much.

"Here we are," Luna said with a flourish. "Tribal Headquarters."

Clark looked around. "Wow," he said. "I'm definitely not in Kansas anymore."

"Well, technically, you are," Luna laughed. "But I know what you mean — it doesn't exactly scream 'home sweet home.' But it's better than sleeping on the streets. C'mon, I'll give you the grand tour." Luna warned Clark to be careful where chunks of the front steps were missing as she led him into the house.

The first floor was just an entryway and a kitchen with an old pot-bellied stove that hadn't been warm in a long time. The second floor, Luna explained, was the junk room. Whoever had been in the house before had stacked all the old, broken furniture and other things to be thrown out there. "We didn't bother to clear it out because the floorboards are rotting," she said, pointing to some caved-in parts. "None of us hangs out here. We mostly stay in the living room on the third floor."

To Clark, the third floor looked like a room that belonged to kids who didn't have a mother around. It was a large space that was cluttered with sleeping bags, clothes, backpacks, CDs, a boombox, unlit candles, someone's teddy bear, candy wrappers, books, pieces of paper. . . . The only thing not covered with stuff was the huge marble fireplace that stood in the middle of the far wall.

Something under a blanket started moving, and out crawled a tiny orange kitten. "Rover!" cried Luna happily. "Come to mommy." The kitten made a beeline for Luna and she scooped it up, kissing the top of its head. "Say hi to Clark."

Clark had to laugh; the kitten had the loudest purr he'd ever heard. He gently scratched the kitten's head, and it gave a little squeak. "She likes you," Luna said.

"She doesn't look much like a 'Rover,' though," Clark said.

"Well, it's better than 'Fluffy,'" Luna said, grinning. "You can leave your stuff here — we'll clear a space for you later."

The fourth floor was where the only working bathroom was — sort of. There was, by some miracle, running water, but none that was hot. "I guess we're lucky it's not winter yet, huh?" Clark asked, wondering how anyone could live here at all, yet remembering what Luna had said about sleeping on the streets.

"Other people have fantasies of being famous," Luna said, gesturing toward the huge claw-foot bathtub. "I dream of having a hot bath some day. And now, I'll show you the best part of the house."

Up two more flights of rickety stairs and through a heavy metal door was the roof, and Clark immediately saw why Luna liked it — the view of Metropolis was incredible. So many buildings, all different shapes and sizes, helicopters buzzing around. . . . Seeing the city this way, it looked exciting and full of possibilities.

Clark smiled. "I'm impressed."

"Wait till you see it at night, when it's all lit up," Luna said. "It's really beautiful. Especially that one," she said, pointing to a tall glass skyscraper.

Clark recognized it immediately as the Luthor-Corp building. It was where Clark's mother went to work when Lionel Luthor had business in Metropolis. As thrilling and weird and new as his journey had been so far, Clark felt a huge, sudden pang of homesickness.

☙ ☙ ☙ ☙

Out of the corner of her eye, Lana Lang could tell that Lex Luthor had just walked into the Talon. He had the kind of confident stride that announced to everyone that he was the owner of the coffee bar, not to mention the guy whose father owned half the town.

Lana was used to Lex dropping by to collect the week's receipts, but she knew he wasn't there on business today. "Have you heard from Clark?" she asked.

"No," Lex said. "Have you?"

Lana shook her head. "His parents called this morning to ask if I knew anything. At first, I didn't believe he'd run away. I went to school thinking he'd show up, but . . . Where do you think he could be?"

Lex sat on a stool at the counter. "My guess is he didn't go far. Metropolis is the nearest big city, easy to get to, easy to get lost in. Actually . . ." He paused, forming an idea. "I have some business I need to attend to in Metropolis. I was going to go next week, but maybe I'll move that trip up a bit."

A determined expression came to Lana's face. "You know, I've been planning to visit my Aunt Nell in Metropolis," she said. "Maybe now would be a good time."

Lex smiled. "The fastest way to get there is by helicopter," he said, rising to leave. "We'll give Clark until tonight — maybe he'll come to his senses and go home. If not, I'll send my car for you first thing tomorrow morning."

CHAPTER 9

Night fell, and as it did the rough neighborhood looked even darker and scarier outside. But inside, Luna lit candles around the room, filling it with a warm glow.

"Hey moon girlie," said a voice at the doorway. "What's up?"

"Skunk!" Luna smiled. "Come meet my new friend Clark."

Clark was startled by the boy who came over to shake his hand. He had a tall, spiky blond Mohawk that was all the more shocking against his tan skin. His merry, almond-shaped brown eyes were framed by a pierced eyebrow, multiple-pierced ears, and a pierced lip that was spread wide in a grin. He was wearing a black leather jacket and a T-shirt with what looked like the name of a punk rock band on it, studded wrist-bands, and jeans torn in six different places. The kid looked totally menacing, but he was so good-natured that Clark couldn't help but think there was truly no way to judge a book by its cover.

"Hey, new dude!" Skunk said, shaking Clark's hand warmly. "Welcome to the Tribe."

"Thanks," Clark said, trying not to stare at all of Skunk's piercings.

"Any luck finding a job today?" Luna asked.

"Nope. But some tourists who wanted to take my picture gave me five bucks." Skunk grinned.

One by one, the other kids who lived in the abandoned house came home. There was Aubrey, a red-haired, freckle-faced guy from Atlanta who, Luna explained, had run away from a foster home. Then there was Margaret, whom everyone called Mag and who was almost as striking as Skunk with her pale pink skin, blue eyes, and white blond hair. Mag was painfully shy, and no one except for maybe Aubrey, who had become her boyfriend, really knew where she came from or why she'd left.

"And me, I came from Miami, like Luna here," Skunk explained as the others shifted their sleeping bags and possessions to make room for Clark. "My folks are real old-school Japanese, so they weren't down with their son's form of self-expression." He laughed, though not with much joy. "What about you, new dude? What's your story?"

"Shouldn't you be out finding the Tribe something for dinner instead of having story hour?" growled a raspy voice.

Clark turned to see a guy who seemed a little older than the others, standing in the doorway. He was almost as tall as Clark, and his dirty white T-shirt showed him to be thin, but muscular. He carried a construction hat, and his electric-blue eyes flashed from Skunk to Clark, then rested on Luna. "Bring home another stray?" he asked as he walked into the room. He didn't sit with the rest, but loomed over them.

"Sean, this is Clark," Luna said.

Clark stood up. "Hey," he said, holding out his hand. Sean ignored it.

"I found him at the bus station," Luna continued in a steady voice. "He needed a place to stay."

"We've got a lot of people here and hardly enough space or food to go around as it is, Luna," Sean said.

"I'm going to get a job, if that's what the problem is," Clark said. Sean looked at Clark, acknowledging him for the first time. The two sized each other up; Sean seemed like the type who like to intimidate, and he didn't like it that Clark wasn't being intimidated. Clark looked back at him innocently, but didn't break his gaze.

Finally, Sean spoke. "That's a good idea. If you want to live with the Tribe, you've got to contribute. Food or money, whatever you can come by. We all take turns providing for everyone. And," he said, returning his withering gaze to Skunk, "I believe it's your turn, Skunk boy."

"No problem," Skunk said, jumping to his feet. "Want to come with me, new dude?"

"Sure," Clark said. He didn't want to leave Luna with this Sean guy, but he sensed that maybe he should get out of his way. At least, for now.

⊛ ⊛ ⊛ ⊛

Jonathan and Martha Kent sat silently at their kitchen table, untouched cups of coffee growing cold in front of them.

It had been a long and jarring day. The discovery of Clark's note had sent them both into a panic. Their son, run away? It wasn't like him at all. But then they remembered their conversation of the night before and realized that Clark must have heard them talking. At that point Martha had dissolved in tears, but Jonathan's guilt was pushed aside by a more pressing matter.

"I'm not sure what we should do now," he had said.

"What do you mean, *what we should do?* We have to call the police, we have to find him!" Martha had been nearly hysterical.

Jonathan steadied her with his good hand, his other arm aching in its sling. "Of course we have to find him. But . . ."

"But *what?*"

Jonathan had worriedly paced the kitchen, trying to work through the thoughts as they came to him. "All his life, we've been trying to keep him from being noticed so no one would find out about his abilities, so they wouldn't take him away from us to study him, exploit him," he'd said. "If we call the sheriff, he'll have no choice but to call the FBI — Clark's a minor. What if . . . what if when they find him, they somehow find out about what he can do?"

Martha's face went from grief to shock as the implications of what Jonathan was saying sank in.

"We could lose him forever," Jonathan had intoned numbly.

They bought some time to think by first calling all of Clark's friends to see if he'd gone to any of their houses, or if he'd said something to anyone. Each time, the answer was no. By then it was late morning, Clark would have been marked absent from school. Martha looked sharply at Jonathan.

"I know that physically he can't get hurt,"

she'd said in a trembling voice. "And I know we have a secret that needs to be kept. But right now, he's a sixteen-year-old boy, he's out there somewhere, and I want him back here! Safe! With us!"

His face etched with apprehension, Jonathan nodded and dialed the sheriff's office. "Ethan? It's Jonathan Kent. I . . . Clark is missing."

The sheriff had come over and talked to them about why Clark might have left. They told him as much as they knew, leaving out the part about Clark's involvement in Jonathan's injuries. Then he'd gone to issue a missing person report and check all the airports, bus stations, and roads in the area. Jonathan and Martha wanted to go out and search for their son, but the sheriff advised them to stay home in case Clark called or returned.

Now it was dinnertime, and the usual family scene of the three of them at the table, passing food and the stories of their day back and forth, was replaced by two people who sat in miserable silence, waiting.

CHAPTER 10

Clark followed Skunk as they walked through the neighborhood. "What's with that guy?" asked Clark. "Did I do something wrong?"

"Sean's not the friendliest dude in the world," Skunk answered. "I ignore him, mostly. I don't even know that much about him. Came from Gotham City, been on his own for a long time. I think he even did some time in a juvenile hall. But he's the one who found the only abandoned building in the neighborhood that's safe enough to live in, and he started the Tribe when he found Aubrey sleeping in the bus station. So he can't be all bad . . . Here we are."

They'd stopped in front of a pay phone down the street from a pizzeria. "Got some change?"

Skunk asked. Clark fished in his pocket and found some, and Skunk dialed the number in the pizzeria window.

"Hi, can I place an order that I'll come and pick up, please?" he said. "One large pizza with ham, pineapple, onions, and anchovies. I'll be by in about ten minutes. Thanks."

Clark made a face. "Is that a standard order for the Tribe?"

"No, dude, that's just it," Skunk explained. "You order a pizza that they can't resell — nobody wants that kind of junk on it. When nobody comes to get it, after a half hour, they've got no choice but to dump it. That's where we come in." Skunk pointed to a Dumpster around the corner from the pizza place.

Clark was about to insist that he'd just pay for a plain pizza. It was bad enough to put all those gross things on it and then pull it out of the garbage, but this was — well, it wasn't *like* stealing, it *was* stealing. Then he realized that he'd been so distracted by Sean's harshness that he'd left his wallet in his knapsack back at the building. At least he knew it would be safe with Luna.

"Skunk, this isn't right," Clark said. "I'll go back to the house and get some money, and we'll just —"

"Dude, if you've got money, hang on to it," Skunk pleaded. "You might not get a job right away, and none of us ever has more than spare change. I know the pizza scheme isn't going to win me any points in heaven, but I feel like we should save any money we've got for important stuff, like medicine if someone gets sick. You don't understand yet 'cause you're new, but you will."

Clark considered what Skunk said. He didn't like what they were doing, but he had to admit that Skunk was right — any money they had should probably be saved for emergencies.

"Okay, just this once," Clark warned. "After this, I'll pay, we'll find the money, or I won't eat."

"We've done that enough times, believe me," Skunk sighed. "But I respect what you're saying."

Skunk told Clark to keep out of sight as they waited in the alley by the Dumpster. After about a half hour, just as Skunk had predicted, a guy walked out with a large bag of garbage in one hand and a pizza box in the other. He hoisted the garbage into the full Dumpster, then threw the box on top. It slid off and behind the giant metal box.

"No!" Skunk hissed.

They waited until the man was gone, then ran to the Dumpster. "Oh man," Skunk said despairingly. There was the pizza box, settled on the ground in the few inches of space between the huge Dumpster and a brick wall.

"Can you reach it?" asked Clark.

Skunk tried to get his arm in. "I can't. It's in too far."

"Let's push this thing out, then."

Skunk stood up and sighed. "Dude, these things weigh a ton when they're empty. And this one's fully loaded." He turned and started to walk away.

Clark braced one hand against the wall and pushed the Dumpster away with the other. Skunk was right; it did weigh more than a ton. Luckily for Clark that wasn't heavy at all. It moved with a loud groan.

Skunk whirled around. "Dude . . . ! How did you do that?"

Thinking fast, Clark pointed down. "See all the pizza grease under the wheels?" he said. "It's not great for your face, but it makes a good lubricant."

Skunk clapped his hands and dove behind the Dumpster to rescue the pizza. He grinned all the way home and told the Tribe that Clark was the true provider that night. Clark almost wished Skunk hadn't told them since, by the time they'd gotten back, the pizza was cold, the cheese had slid to one side, and it was impossible to pick out the mismatched toppings. It was one of the grossest things Clark had ever eaten, yet the Tribe all thanked him for it. All except for Sean.

After dinner, Luna produced a spare sleeping bag that had been left behind by a former Tribe member. She cleared a spot by her own near the fireplace and helped Clark settle in. Sean snatched up his sleeping bag, grumbling that it was too crowded in there for him, and stomped down the stairs to the second floor. No one tried to stop him.

Clark rubbed his eyes. He was so tired from all that had happened. Last night he'd been in his room in Smallville, preparing to run away from parents who loved him and the only home he'd ever known. Tonight, he was sleeping on the floor of an abandoned building in Metropolis next to a girl with an orange kitten curled up beside her and a mysterious glow in her eyes.

One by one the candles were blown out, and all Clark could see as he lay on the floor was Luna smiling at him.

"Welcome to the Tribe," she whispered.

❦ ❦ ❦ ❦

"Excuse me, but are you really doing this? And why?"

Lana stopped packing her suitcase for a moment and sighed. "Chloe, I don't know why, but I feel like I have to go to Metropolis to look for

Clark. It's so unlike him to do something like this."

"Granted, running away is extremely un-Clark-like behavior, but so is you splitting school to go to Metropolis with Lex Luthor," Chloe said, sitting cross-legged on Lana's bed.

Last year, when Lana's Aunt Nell had decided to move to Metropolis with her fiancé, Dean, Lana was desperate not to leave her friends, the Talon, or Smallville. Luckily, Chloe and Mr. Sullivan had invited Lana to move in with them. It was so ironic, Chloe thought; she'd always been a little jealous of Lana, who was gorgeous, popular, and her number one competition for Clark. Yet she and Lana had ended up becoming best friends, maybe even closer than Chloe had been with Clark.

Lana's move into the Sullivan household was easier when it turned out that Chloe's fears of a possible Clark-Lana romance hadn't been realized. Somehow, things had gone south between Clark and Lana, and although Chloe wanted both of her friends to be happy, she didn't necessarily want them to be happy *together*.

But this afternoon, Lana had come home from the Talon, gone straight to her room, and begun packing to go search for Clark. Chloe herself was concerned about him — he was still her friend, after all . . . *Yeah, right,* a part of her heart suddenly piped up. *You're still in love with Clark and always will be. You're just jealous because Lana can run off and look for him, and Dad will never let you go too.*

"I mean," Chloe said, trying to derail her own train of thought, "I can't believe your aunt is even okay with this!"

Lana, meanwhile, had gone back to packing determinedly. "She's just so thrilled that I want to come and visit, she doesn't care how I'm getting there or why." She didn't look at Chloe as she answered.

Chloe was curious by nature — it was how she'd uncovered all the strange things that happened around Smallville, and why she wrote about them in the school newspaper, the *Torch*. She prided herself on being able to read between the lines, and right now it seemed like Lana had some unspoken reason for wanting to look for Clark. It was almost like she *needed* to look for him. And Chloe, who knew she wasn't anywhere near getting close to Clark the way she wanted to, felt those old jealous emotions rising up in her throat. She remembered encouraging Lana to finally have that talk with Clark, and she mentally kicked herself; she'd told Lana not to run away from her feelings, and now it appeared that Lana was actually taking her advice.

"Lana," she asked hesitantly, not really wanting to hear the answer, "did something happen between you and Clark?"

"Yes," Lana said, snapping her suitcase closed. "But I don't want to talk about it."

Chapter 11

Clark had hardly slept at all the night before, between lying on the floor and hearing the strange creaks and groans of the old house, as well as the unfamiliar sounds of the city outside. Yet he'd still woken up at the crack of dawn. *You can take the boy off the farm,* he thought, *but you can't take the farm out of the boy.* Clark stopped brushing his teeth for a moment. That was something his father would have said. *I hope Mom and Dad aren't too upset,* he thought.

He hadn't even been away from home for more than a day, but his parents were never far from his thoughts. Even though they knew nothing could hurt him, it never stopped them from worrying about him. Clark knew they were probably going crazy wondering where he was, and his impulse was to run right home just to reassure them.

But then he remembered all the reasons he'd run away in the first place. *I probably did the right thing by leaving*, he thought, even though he missed his mother and father, not to mention Pete, Chloe, and Lana.

Just then, Luna came into the bathroom wearing a big sweatshirt over her pajama pants, her wild hair tamed for the moment in a ponytail. Clark quickly rinsed his mouth and grabbed a towel. "Hey," he said with a smile.

"Good morning," she said, grinning back at him. "I was hoping I'd catch you before you left."

"Yeah, I figured I'd get an early start," Clark said. "I want to see if I can find a job today."

"You will," Luna said with certainty. "I had a dream about it last night."

"Really?"

She nodded. "I saw the word 'Mercury,' and you were running really fast. Like, faster than a human being could possibly run."

Before Clark could stop himself, his jaw had dropped open a bit. "I know that sounds weird,"

76

Luna said, "but believe me, it had something to do with you finding a job." She edged out the door. "I'll just go downstairs until you're done."

"It's okay, I'm done," Clark said, pulling himself together. After all, what she'd said had just been a coincidence, nothing more. "The bathroom's all yours. So . . . I guess I'll see you tonight?"

"I'll be here. And hopefully we'll have something a little better for dinner," she smiled. "Oh, hey, I almost forgot — I have something for you." In her hand was a length of black cord; tied to the end was what looked like a small green stone.

Instinctively, Clark drew back — a meteorite? But he felt no pain, no wave of agony, as Luna stood on her tiptoes behind him and tied the cord around his neck. "What is it?" he asked.

"Beach glass," she replied. "Broken glass gets smoothed down by the sand while it's surfing around in the ocean, and it looks like little colored stones when it washes up on the shore. I used to collect it at home," she said.

Clark rubbed the smooth edge of the glass with his fingers. "I thought it was — something else," he said as he looked at it in the mirror.

"Like jade?" Luna smiled. "Sorry, but if I had anything that valuable, I'd probably sell it."

"This is better," Clark said. "Thank you."

"There," Luna said, finishing the knot and wrapping her arms around Clark's shoulders to give him a hug. "That's for luck and prosperity."

"Really?" Clark said, thrilled that she wasn't letting go. He held on to her hands as they rested on his chest. "A piece of glass can do all that?"

Luna's arms slowly fell away from Clark's shoulders. He wasn't sure, but as he looked at their reflections in the huge bathroom mirror, he thought he saw something in Luna's eyes shut down. Or, actually, shut him out. "Um . . . well, that's what I hear — you know, old superstitions," she said. "You'd better get going if you want to find that job."

Reluctantly, Clark turned to leave. "You're right," he said. "Oh, and I almost forgot — your bath is ready."

Luna smiled at him. "Very funny," she said. She turned to look at the bathtub, which was full of . . . wait, was the water steaming? It couldn't

be — there hadn't been hot water in this building in forever . . .

She dipped her hand in; the water was won-
derfully, soothingly hot.

"Clark?!" she called excitedly. But he was already gone.

☙ ☙ ☙ ☙

Lex loved the way people snapped to attention
when he walked into the offices of LuthorCorp.
"Good morning, Mr. Luthor," said the receptionist and a dozen other people who seemed to want
to get out of his way quickly as he walked com-
mandingly down the hall. It was interesting — he
never shouted or threatened like his father did,
yet the people who worked for LuthorCorp
seemed to have an instinctual fear of him. He had
to admit he liked that.

"Good morning, Mr. Luthor."

"Is it, Trumble?" Lex asked, stretching his arms
across the doorway of a small office. *Trapped*, he
thought, amusing himself for a moment before

he walked into the office and got down to business. "I don't know if *I'm* having a good morning."

"I-I'm not sure what you mean, Mr. Luthor," Mr. Trumble said, hoping he wasn't sweating noticeably.

Lex sat comfortably in the chair opposite Mr. Trumble's desk. "I haven't heard from our lawyers yet about the proposed site for the chemical plant downtown. Are those buildings historic landmarks or aren't they?"

Hal Trumble swallowed. "My group's not finished negotiating with the Metropolis Zoning Board," he said.

"You were the one who sold my father on that site, Trumble. The demolition and construction crews are ready, and my father won't be happy if those buildings are still standing by next week." He had to hide a smile as he watched the man try not to squirm.

"I'll tell you what I *have* heard," Lex continued. "Rumors of corruption, bribery, and other illegal methods of getting this deal done." He walked around Mr. Trumble's desk and stood behind him. "You wouldn't know anything about that, would you?"

Craning his neck uncomfortably to face Lex, Mr. Trumble said, "No, Mr. Luthor. I haven't heard anything like that."

Lex considered torturing him some more, but decided to let him go. It was unlikely that this nervous little man would be behind the corruption Lex was talking about.

"Well then," he said, benevolently patting Trumble on the shoulder, "if you do hear something, see to it that you inform me immediately."

Lex could have sworn he heard the man sigh with relief as he walked out the door.

❧ ❧ ❧ ❧

It was late in the afternoon, and Clark was tired and discouraged. Walking around Metropolis looking for a job made his farm chores seem easy, and he'd heard the words "no" and "sorry" more times in this one afternoon than he had in his entire life.

So far, he'd looked for work at countless clothing stores, a bunch of diners and pizza places, and even a construction site or two. Either they didn't need any help or, understandably, they didn't want to risk hiring someone who was underage with no permanent address. Now Clark was just wandering aimlessly. He would never make enough money to help pay for the tractor at this rate, and if he couldn't get a job he was just worrying his parents needlessly.

So much for Luna's dream, he thought as he touched the green beach glass she'd tied around his neck. He hoped she wouldn't be disappointed in him —

Clark stopped dead in his tracks, unable to believe where he'd wandered. He stood in front of a bustling storefront with a sign that read: MERCURY MESSENGERS — FASTEST IN METROPOLIS.

It was just as Luna had said. Clark couldn't figure out how she'd known, but it didn't matter — as he walked inside, he knew he was in the right place. Now all he had to do was convince whoever was in charge.

It didn't seem like it was going to be easy. The

dispatcher, whose desk nameplate read C. GRIMES, was an older man who hadn't shaved in days and had an unlit cigar clamped in the corner of his jaws. He ignored Clark completely as he barked addresses and instructions into three different walkie-talkies and five phones.

"Excuse me, sir," Clark finally said.

The man looked up at him as if daring him to continue.

"Um, I was hoping you could give me a job," Clark said.

Mr. Grimes put down one of the phones. "Listen, kid, I've got all the messengers I need. Rico, where are you?" he barked into a walkie-talkie. "I got a rush pickup for you right now!"

"I really need the work," Clark said. "I'm kind of desperate."

"You look it, kid, and my heart's breaking. But I'm a little busy —"

"I'm really fast," Clark insisted.

"Then you can get *out* of here fast," the dispatcher snarled. "Rico! Where the hell —"

Clark boldly leaned over the desk. "Sir, the way I see it, I need this job and you need somebody to do it. I guarantee I'll be the fastest messenger you'll ever have. Just give me this one job you need done right now, and if I don't get the package where it's going in record time, you don't have to pay me."

Mr. Grimes clicked off his walkie-talkie and switched the cigar stub to the other side of his mouth. "Your bike parked outside?"

"I . . . don't have a bike," Clark said, hoping the man wouldn't ask any more questions about how he was going to get around.

The dispatcher leaned over the desk and looked at Clark's work boots. "You're not even wearing sneakers." Clark shifted uncomfortably but kept his expression serious.

"Remind me that I gave you a chance when I'm kicking your butt around the block," Mr. Grimes said with a growl. "Get to the messenger center of the Grand Building at Fourth and Main. They'll tell you where to take the package."

"Consider it done," said Clark. He trotted out of the building, but once he was outside, he sped things up.

CHAPTER 12

As part owner of the Talon, I hope I'm not overstepping my employer-employee boundaries here," Lex said, "but you look absolutely beautiful."

At the end of a frustrating day that had turned up no sign of Clark or of the corruption at LuthorCorp, Lex had suggested that he and Lana have dinner. Lana blushed and looked down at the dress she'd borrowed from Nell. It was a good thing she'd dressed up a little, because Lex had taken her to the most elegant Japanese restaurant in Metropolis.

Lex was vaguely aware that he might be staring at Lana, but it was hard not to. He'd always understood why Clark was in love with her, but tonight, in her pink silk dress and strappy sandals, Lana was breathtaking. Fortunately, Lex was distracted by the waitress, who came over with their orders.

The waitress was also eye-catching, but for completely different reasons. Her pretty features lost a battle for attention to her pure white hair, pink skin, and light blue eyes. She was an albino, a person born without any of the pigment that would give her hair and skin color — a random fluke of genes that happens in nature. Lex was reminded of seeing an albino snake in a zoo once when he was a child, and he'd thought it looked really cool. But for someone to have to go to school looking so unlike everyone else . . .

Lex knew what it felt like to be different from years of the other kids at boarding school teasing him for being bald. On good days, he'd tried to tell himself he was special, and that his baldness meant he'd been singled out, meant for greatness somehow. On his bad days, Lex had just felt like a freak. *She's probably been called that too*, he thought, *and worse*.

He smiled at the waitress, trying to give her a sort of secret handshake with his eyes. She smiled back before she left, though so shyly and quickly he wasn't sure she'd understood.

"Wow," Lana said, looking at her tray of sushi. "It's so pretty I almost don't want to eat it."

"If you don't, the chef will think he's been dishonored in some way and commit hara-kiri," Lex said, smiling.

"Well, we don't want that," Lana said, picking up her chopsticks. "This is all so nice, I could almost forget why we're really here." She looked down at her food but still didn't eat.

"You're worried about him," Lex said.

"Of course I am," Lana said. "Who knows where he is, or what he's doing? We don't even know if he's really here."

"It's a logical choice. It's where I'd come if I were Clark."

Lana looked off into the distance. "If I were Clark . . . It's funny. I've known Clark Kent almost all my life, and lately I've been feeling like I don't really know him at all."

"Clark's not an easy person to be friends with, is he?" Lex asked abruptly.

Lana hesitated. "What do you mean?"

"He's a little . . . secretive sometimes."

"You noticed that too." Lana laughed. "I thought it was just me."

Lex leaned back and sipped his green tea. "Clark doesn't share himself easily with anyone. But he certainly seems to want to with you."

Lana looked down. "That's not — Clark and I are friends. Just friends."

"Was that your choice, or his?"

"It was mutual," Lana said, more defensively than she'd wanted to.

"Well, you never know," Lex said. "That situation might work itself out someday."

Lana pushed her food around with her chopsticks. "I don't think so," she said. "Clark is my friend, and for whatever reasons, I think that's all he can be to me."

Lex smiled. "You're only sixteen, Lana," he said. He'd fixed his penetrating gaze on her again, yet he seemed almost to be talking to himself. "You have no idea how much people can change."

It had been over an hour since Lex had dropped
Lana off at her Aunt Nell's apartment, yet Lana
had spent nearly all that time just looking out the
big picture window in the living room and thinking. It seemed ironic to Lana that it should have a
great view of the LuthorCorp building, but then
again, most of Metropolis probably did, since it
was the tallest building in the city.

Aunt Nell and Dean were asleep by the time
Lana got back to the apartment, and she was
grateful for some time alone. She gazed out at the
city lights, amazed at how many of them were on
at this time of night. Metropolis was a big place,
and Lana wondered whether Clark was all right,
what he was doing right at that moment. If he
was even there.

And what am I doing here? Lana asked herself.
Obviously, she'd come because Clark was a good
friend, despite what she'd said to him at the
Talon. Just the memory of that awful conversation made Lana cringe.

But there was something else that Lana didn't want to admit to herself: the possibility that she'd come to Metropolis looking for Clark out of guilt. *I'm part of the reason he left,* she thought. *He needed me, and I turned him away. Maybe if I hadn't, he'd still be back home, up in his hayloft, looking up at the stars like he always does.*

But, part of her mind argued, hadn't she been pushing aside her feelings for Clark long enough? Didn't she have a right to tell him how frustrated she felt about their relationship? Especially after that time . . .

Pain warmed to anger as Lana remembered the few days where it seemed like Clark, who'd always been a little different, had completely lost his mind. He'd come to school on his father's motorcycle wearing a black leather jacket — very out of character for Clark. He'd flirted wildly with a new girl at school, changing overnight from the shy guy he had always been. Then he'd walked into the Talon and kissed Lana.

That kiss. The memory of it still tugged at Lana. Whenever she had allowed herself to wonder what it would be like if she and Clark were together, she'd always imagined that his kisses would be gentle, affectionate, sweet.

But on that day, he had kissed her passionately, with a confidence — almost an arrogance — she hadn't thought he was capable of. It was as if he thought he had the power to take anything he wanted — including her — and nothing could stand in his way. Lana frowned. That attitude reminded her of someone else . . .

Lex Luthor. It seemed like she'd been describing Lex, not Clark.

But it *had* been Clark. And then, just a day later, he'd come looking for her with flowers, trying to apologize and explain that he hadn't been himself.

Well, Lana thought with frustration, *he explained as much as he would*. Which, when it came to Clark Kent, was never enough.

A light flicked on in a large office at the top of the LuthorCorp skyscraper. Lana wondered if people really worked all night in this city. Was it Lex, searching for whatever had brought him here?

Lana had known Lex for a little over a year, but she still couldn't figure him out. He seemed to have two sides: one, well-meaning, the other . . . well, as Clark's father always said, he was a Luthor. There was something slightly shady about him. But Lana would never be able to hold that against him; she would always feel indebted to Lex for helping her save the Talon and for being such a good friend to Clark.

Lana closed the window shade, shutting out the waning moon and the glow of the Luthor-Corp building. She had made flyers with Clark's photo on them and a number to call if anyone had seen him, and if she was going to put them up around the city tomorrow she'd better get some rest tonight.

Besides, sleeping was far preferable to staying up and wondering how she could feel so drawn to someone, yet have so many questions that pushed her away.

CHAPTER 13

"Hey Mag!" said Skunk, beaming hopefully. "What's in the bags?"

Mag just smiled as she spread several takeout containers in the middle of the floor. The Tribe excitedly sat down in a circle and looked at them hungrily.

"Okay," she said. "This is eel and cucumber, and these are spicy tuna rolls. Oh, here are some California rolls . . ."

"Yay Mag!" Skunk laughed. "She rules! She is the queen provider!" Mag blushed deeply as Aubrey kissed her cheek.

"Mag has a friend who works at this fancy-schmancy Japanese restaurant," Luna explained to Clark. "She couldn't do her shift tonight, so Mag got it instead."

"And they gave me all the leftovers to take home," Mag said from behind her white bangs. "But that's not the best part. I waited on this rich guy and his girlfriend, and do you know how much he tipped me?" Everyone waited. *"Fifty bucks!"*

"Yay Rich Guy, whoever he is!" Skunk shouted, and everyone clapped and laughed. No one mentioned it, but everyone knew the mood was definitely lighter when Sean wasn't around.

Clark surveyed the takeout containers on the floor, searching for anything that looked even vaguely familiar. "Are we actually eating raw fish for dinner?" he whispered to Luna. He didn't want to appear ungrateful for Mag's contribution, but the idea of eating something uncooked and wrapped in seaweed wasn't appealing to a guy who'd been brought up on things like roast chicken, meat loaf, and spaghetti.

"You've *never* had sushi?" Luna asked, surprised. "Oh Clark, it's really good!"

"I'm from a farm in Smallville," Clark said with a shrug. "I guess we just didn't have raw fish every Sunday night like other people."

"Go ahead, Clark, try it," Skunk said. "You might like it. And even if you don't, it won't kill you."

Clark managed a half smile. "That's true," he said, reaching for an eel roll. Hesitantly, he put it in his mouth. Luna looked at him expectantly. "Well?"

"Mmm," Clark mumbled. "Just like mom never used to make."

❧ ❧ ❧

"Luna, how come you can't see any stars here?"

Clark and Luna were sitting on the roof, watching the moon rise and the city flicker to life like a thousand fireflies. He'd been telling her about getting a job at Mercury Messengers, about how he'd delivered the package he was sent to pick up so fast that the dispatcher called the recipient to make sure he wasn't lying. But then the dispatcher had actually smiled and told Clark to report to work first thing in the morning.

"It's pretty strange, the way you dreamed the whole thing," Clark had said, half-asking her how she'd known, without coming right out and saying it. But Luna just smiled.

As it had gotten darker, Clark had waited for the stars to come out, but the city's sky was a strangely blank canvas. "At home, you can see tons of stars, all the constellations . . ." he said.

Luna shrugged. "I could see them back home in Miami, too. I think there's too much light and pollution here. Don't worry, Clark," she said, patting his arm. "They're still up there, watching over you." Clark smiled; it was a comforting thought.

"Okay, now tell me," Luna demanded. "How did you make the bathwater hot this morning?"

"Only if you tell me how you knew I was going to get a job at Mercury," Clark answered.

Luna looked down at her hands. "That's kind of a secret," she said. "You know, just like you have a secret."

Immediately, Clark's guard went up. "What do you mean?"

"Why you left home," Luna said. "Everybody in the Tribe has a reason for being here, but sometimes it's something they can't share. But that's okay with me, Clark. I understand."

"Thank you for that," Clark said, inwardly relaxing. He was so used to having to hide, and it was a relief not to have to try to explain something away. "I don't mean to be secretive," he continued. "There's just not much about me to know."

"Yeah, right. I'll bet there's nothing interesting about you," Luna said sarcastically, gently nudging Clark with her shoulder. "Wait — let me see if I can guess." Luna took a deep breath and seemed to be concentrating on Clark, studying him. It felt like she was looking right into him. After a moment, Luna said, "You're adopted."

"I am," Clark said with surprise, though it could have been a lucky guess.

"And . . . you found out last year."

"No," Clark said, "I've always known I was adopted."

Luna frowned. "There was something that you found out last year, something about who you are or where you came from."

Slowly it dawned on Clark that Luna wasn't guessing at all. Somehow she was picking up the truth — he *had* discovered something about himself last year, when his father showed him the spaceship he'd fallen to Earth in. *But how can she know this?* he wondered, feeling that prickly nervousness he got whenever someone was coming close to guessing that he wasn't what he seemed.

But Luna didn't push it. "Oh, well. Do you know who your birth parents are, Clark? Or where they're from?"

Clark shook his head, resisting the impulse to look up at the sky.

"Do you want to know?" Luna asked, taking out a deck of cards from her jacket pocket.

Clark smiled dubiously. "The story of my life is in those cards?"

"You'd be surprised what these will tell you," Luna said. As she shuffled the deck, she asked, "Who is Clark Kent?" She put the cards down and cut the deck, taking cards off the top and putting the bottom half on top of those. Then she picked up a card. "That's funny," she said, turning it around so he could see. "It's The Star."

Clark stared at the card, which had a drawing of glowing stars over a woman who knelt by a stream. He'd never seen a card like it before. "I don't get it," he said. "What are these?"

"My tarot cards?" she asked. "They kind of help you find out about yourself, about stuff that's coming up, things like that."

"So what does The Star mean?" Clark asked.

"It has to do with the universe — see the seven stars? They represent the seven planets that go with astrological signs. And it's a card that corresponds with the element of air." Luna laughed. "Did you fall down from the sky, Clark?"

Clark laughed too, though uneasily. This was weird.

"Let me see if I can get a little more information," Luna said. Clark was about to ask her what she meant, but he just watched as she looked at the card. Luna's eyes became hazy, like she was staring off into the distance. She was quiet for a moment or two, and when her eyes came back into focus, she looked at him, confused. "Strange."

"What?" Clark asked.

"All I saw were these green rocks shooting around," Luna said.

Clark swallowed hard. *Meteor rocks.*

"Does that mean anything to you?" Luna asked.

"Um . . . not really," was all Clark could think of to say. He didn't understand how Luna knew these things about him, and he was desperate to change the subject before she found a card that had a spaceship on it or something. "Hey, I don't know much about you either," he said. "Will those tell me?"

"Sure," Luna smiled, handing him the cards. "But don't ask out loud. Just think about the question while you shuffle, and pull one card — that'll be your 'answer.' I don't want any accusations that I fixed it somehow." She laughed in a way that told Clark it had probably happened to her before.

He picked up the cards and looked at the strange pictures on them. He didn't really believe these cards could reveal secrets about people or predict the future. *But then again,* he thought, *who would believe a guy could come from another planet, be super strong, and have the ability to see through walls?* Besides, he liked Luna and didn't want to hurt her feelings.

Clark smiled to himself. If he didn't have to ask the question out loud, he could ask anything he wanted . . . He closed his eyes and shuffled the cards. When he was done, he halved the deck, just as Luna had, and picked one from the top. He stared at the card, recognizing its obvious meaning, but he didn't turn it around for Luna to see.

She raised her eyebrows. "Well? Which one did you get?"

The card Clark held in his hand was The Lovers. "Sorry, can't tell you that," he said, blushing deeply. He quickly put it back in the deck, covering it with the other cards.

"O-*kaaay,*" Luna said, laughing, "but did it answer your question?"

"Uh, yeah," Clark said. "But no more cards for me tonight."

"All right, no more cards," Luna said, taking Clark's hand in hers. "Palms instead." Clark was about to protest, but the feeling of her fingers slowly tracing the lines on his hand sent warm shivers through his body, and he didn't want her to stop.

"Let's see . . . you've got a really strong lifeline. There will be two great loves in your life . . . and one great enemy, someone close to you. And . . ."

Luna looked up at Clark, her face only inches away from his. "Actually, I'm not that good at reading palms. I was just kind of looking for an excuse to hold your hand," she said with a shy smile.

Clark gave in to the magnetic pull that drew him closer to Luna. He'd so rarely experienced that great feeling that someone who you really wanted to kiss actually wanted to kiss you, too. And this time, there was no boyfriend, no threatened friendship, nothing to keep them apart. Their mouths softly touched and melted together.

Neither of them noticed the squeak of the roof door as it was slowly closed.

CHAPTER 14

Clark woke up to bright fall sunlight shining through the broken windows in the living room. Even after his second day in this place, it took him a moment to remember where he was. Would he ever get used to it — or to spending nights on a hard floor in a sleeping bag?

His mood changed when his eyes fell on Luna, who was sleeping peacefully nearby. He leaned over and gently kissed her cheek. He was surprised to see her there. She said she usually woke up to watch the sunrise from the roof, but they had been up all night, holding each other as the moon and the city lights shone all around them.

Clark smiled as he quietly slipped out of his sleeping bag. He couldn't believe how nice a kiss, or even just holding someone's hand, could feel when it was with the right person. It made him realize how out of sync he'd been with the girls he knew. He thought he'd liked Chloe for a while, but when she suddenly suggested they just go back to being friends, he found he was really okay with that.

And, of course, there was Lana. But their entire friendship-relationship thing seemed to have imploded, so there was no reason to worry about that anymore.

Now he was with a wild-looking but totally sweet girl who seemed to like him just the way he was. No complications, no weirdness. Well, aside from her strange cards and the way she was able to tell things about him. He shrugged it off and smiled as he headed to the stairs with his toothbrush and towel.

"Clark, dude!" Skunk said as he came down the stairs, raising his hand for a high five. "You're looking happy. What's up, man?"

Clark slapped Skunk's palm and shrugged innocently. "Just getting ready to go to work." He was about to walk up to the bathroom when Skunk said, "Um, I don't mean to ruin your day, dude, but Sean's looking for you. He's up in the bathroom." Skunk's face turned serious.

"Fine," Clark said. "Have to brush my teeth anyway." But Skunk took another step toward Clark and spoke in a low voice. "Clark, man, be careful of Sean. He can be kind of a bad dude, you know what I'm saying?"

Clark paused, wondering what this was all about. "Don't worry, Skunk," he said. "I can take care of myself."

Skunk nodded, though his face still showed concern, and then he disappeared into the living room.

❧ ❧ ❧ ❧

Clark went upstairs and found Sean at the huge sink, his face covered in soapy foam. It made him look like a rabid animal. In between strokes of his razor, he took a swig from a bottle of beer.

"Breakfast of champions?" Clark asked sarcastically as he walked in.

Sean turned to face him. "It's noon somewhere, man. Besides, I'm eighteen and . . ." He gave Clark a hard look. "You're not my father."

They stared each other down for a minute. Then Sean went back to shaving and asked, "Skunk tell you I wanted to see you?" Clark nodded. "Good, good," Sean said, sounding very much like a man who had too much power over people. *A bully*, Clark thought as he tried to keep his expression blank, aware that his temper was flaring. Sean just smiled.

"You're a pretty brave guy, Clark," he said. "You just got here and already you're stepping on my territory."

"Excuse me?" Clark said.

"Luna," Sean said. "Don't tell me you didn't know that she and I are together."

Clark hesitated. Luna and Sean? "No," he said, not quite buying it. "I didn't know that."

Sean's glare was steady. "Well, buddy, it's true. Just thought I'd give you a little heads-up. That's not going to be a problem, is it?" Clark shook his head, unsure of what else he could say or do. He didn't believe Sean — *or is it that I don't* want *to believe him?* But if it were true . . . then Luna had lied to him.

"Besides," Sean continued, sensing Clark's inner confusion, "you don't look like the type of guy who'd want to hang with a witch."

Clark was jolted to attention. "A . . . what?"

Sean stopped wiping his face and wore an unconvincing look of surprise. "She didn't tell you that either?" His laugh was a sharp bark. "And you didn't figure it out — the cards, the candles, the 'dreams' — ?" Sean made quote marks in the air with his fingers and laughed again. "Tell me, Clark . . . has she read your palm yet?"

Clark felt his face become hot with anger. He wanted Sean to shut up, and he felt betrayed by Luna. How could she possibly be with this clown? And what was this stuff about her being a witch?

Sean put his arm around Clark's shoulders. "Look, man, it's cool," he said. His tone was friendly, though he couldn't pretend well enough to take the edge out of his voice. "You're new, she put the moves on you, and you didn't know she was with me. But don't worry, Clark. It's all good. We're still buddies." He hit Clark's back with a hard slap as he walked away.

Clark's hands clenched into fists. He so wanted to do something to wipe that false smile off Sean's face, and it burned him to know that he couldn't.

He even managed to resist the urge when Sean turned at the doorway and said, "Oh, one more thing, Clark: be careful around here. This place can be kind of . . . dangerous, you know?"

CHAPTER 15

"Clark! Hey Clark, wait up!"

Pretending not to hear Luna's voice, Clark snatched his messenger bag, trotted down the rickety stairs, and stormed out the front door. Luna had to run to catch up with him, and she stepped in front of him on the stoop to keep him from walking away.

"Hey," she said. "You didn't even say goodbye." She reached up to kiss him, but he turned away.

"I have to get to work," he said.

"Not until you tell me what's wrong."

He didn't want to look at her, afraid his face would show how hurt he was. "Maybe you should ask Sean," he said sulkily.

"I wish *you'd* just talk to me, Clark," Luna said, looking confused. "Please?"

Clark sighed. "You didn't tell me you were . . . with him."

Luna's hands dropped from Clark's shoulders and went to her hips. "That's because I'm *not*," she said.

"Well . . . he seems to think so." Clark searched Luna's face for any hint of guilt. There was none, but now she looked angry.

"Look, Sean may think he's got some kind of right to me because he's the one who rescued me at the bus station," Luna said. Clark understood how meaningful that was for the members of the Tribe; the member who found a person and brought her or him home had a special place in that person's life. "He did for me what I did for you," Luna said, "so in a way, I owe him.

"But," she said sternly, "I've never been with Sean like *that*, and it doesn't mean he owns me. No one does. I choose who I want to be with. And," she said, her voice softening, "that's you."

Relieved, Clark smiled and took Luna's hand. "I'm sorry," he said. "I think I've got 'other guy' syndrome. It's happened before."

"Well, it's not happening now." Luna raised two fingers to her head, saluting him. "Scout's honor," she said, grinning. "Remember?"

Clark nodded. "I remember." He pulled Luna close, wrapping his arms around her as she put her head on his chest. Being with her like this felt so good, he wanted to forget everything that Sean had said. But . . .

"Luna," he began, "there was something else —"

Just then, Luna looked up and shouted, "Clark, watch out!"

He barely had time to look up before a bottle hit him, smashing into a thousand razor-sharp pieces.

"Clark!" Luna cried. "Are you all right?"

The bottle hadn't hurt him at all; the shards just itched a little as they bounced off him. But as Luna gingerly searched Clark's forehead for the gash that should have been there, she sounded bewildered.

"I don't understand," she said, brushing bits of glass out of his hair. "I thought — I could have sworn it was heading straight for you . . ."

Thinking fast, Clark said, "Yeah, I thought so too. But it must've hit here first." He pointed to the stone window ledge he was standing next to. He knew Luna would have flinched instinctively and hadn't seen the bottle actually shattering against his head. "Lucky break, huh?"

Luna looked baffled, but relieved. "Really lucky," she said, hugging Clark. Then she pulled away. "I don't know where that bottle came from, but you kind of smell like beer now."

Clark frowned as he ran a hand over the damp spot in his hair. *Sean.* "Not the best way to show up to work," he said lightly, hiding his rage. "I'm just going to run upstairs and stick my head in the sink."

At first Clark walked into the building, but once out of Luna's sight he sped straight up to the roof, looking for Sean. He was furious, not for himself but because the bottle could've hit Luna. *When I find him . . .*

But he didn't. Sean had just disappeared. Not wanting to be late for work, Clark promised himself he'd deal with Sean later.

CHAPTER 16

In a corner office high in a glass building in midtown Metropolis, a phone rang softly. "Luthor-Corp, Hal Trumble speaking."

"It's me," growled a voice on the other end of the line.

Mr. Trumble turned away from his open door. "I thought I told you not to call me on this line," he whispered anxiously.

"Chill, I'll be fast. I changed my mind. I'm ready to do that job you wanted me to do."

Mr. Trumble smiled. "Meet me tomorrow at noon. You know the place."

"Bring the money. Cash." Mr. Trumble was relieved to hear the *click* that signaled the end of the conversation, and of his problems.

"Trumble," said Lex from the doorway. "Looks like you just got good news. I hope it's something to do with that property downtown."

"It is," Trumble said. "It looks like we're almost ready to go forward."

❧ ❧ ❧

Martha Kent nearly jumped out of her skin when she heard the knock on her kitchen door. Two days with no word from Clark had left both her and Jonathan sleepless and edgy. Not knowing where he was, what he was doing, whether he was eating . . . It had worn her down to a bundle of raw nerves.

She caught her breath when she saw Chloe Sullivan at the door. "Oh, hello, Chloe," she said. "Come on in."

"Sorry if I startled you," Chloe said, putting her book bag on the table and sitting down. "How are you and Mr. Kent, anyway?"

Martha sighed. "Jonathan is resting, only because I threatened to take him back to the hospital if he didn't, and I'm . . . well, you can see how I am. Oh, where are my manners — do you want anything to drink, Chloe?" Mrs. Kent looked like she would welcome any kind of distraction, so Chloe asked for a glass of water.

"I'm guessing you haven't heard anything yet," Chloe said.

Mrs. Kent shook her head. "The police haven't found any leads, either."

"I know," said Chloe. "I've got a friend who works at the sheriff's office. But since I'd like to think I know Clark better than the police do, I've been doing a little checking myself."

"Oh?" Martha was strangely discomforted by Chloe's helpful tone.

"There's not just the question of where he went, but *how* he left town in the first place," Chloe began. "He didn't take either of your cars, so that's out. He didn't take the train because the station's too far to get to without a car, and none of us drove him. So I went to the bus station with a photo of Clark, but nobody saw him there. I even went to see the woman who was on the graveyard shift on Monday night, and she said she would have remembered him. So he didn't leave by bus."

Martha swallowed. As desperate as she was for any clue about her son, this wasn't the way she wanted to get it. Chloe had a habit of pursuing things doggedly. Martha remembered when the kids once had to write a paper about a classmate for homework, and Chloe had practically interrogated the Kents about Clark's adoption — how they'd found him, where, when, and lots of other questions. It had made them very uneasy.

"That leaves a plane," Chloe went on, "and I don't think he would've spent all of his money on a ticket. So he either hitchhiked, or he just walked out of town —"

More like ran, Martha thought.

"— And that hardly seems likely." Chloe just looked at Mrs. Kent with raised eyebrows, as though she was expecting her to fill in the blanks. To Martha, it seemed like Chloe's main reason for finding Clark now was to satisfy her own curiosity. He'd gone from being a friend she cared about to a mystery that had to be solved.

"I don't know what to say," Martha answered honestly.

Frowning, Chloe said, "Mrs. Kent, please don't take this the wrong way, but do you think Clark might have gone to look for his birth parents? I mean, a lot of adopted kids do that — search for their real mother and father. Maybe Clark —"

"I don't think so, Chloe," Martha said in a clipped voice. "His note didn't mention anything like that." She looked down at her fidgeting fingers.

Chloe blushed. "I'm sorry, Mrs. Kent, I didn't meant to . . . I was just trying to help."

"I know, Chloe, and I appreciate it. I just don't think this has anything to do with Clark's adoption."

Chloe knew it was time to leave. She apologized again and let herself out, leaving a worn-looking Mrs. Kent at the table.

Chloe felt bad about hurting her feelings, but as she walked toward her car, she thought again about the file she'd discovered when she had to write that essay about Clark. He'd been the only case handled by an adoption agency based in Metropolis that had closed down after only six months. Very strange.

Clark had been really upset about Chloe poking around in his life, and it had taken a while for her to smooth things out with him. Still, she hadn't been able to bring herself to delete the adoption file from her computer. Or to stop wondering why he always seemed to be so evasive about himself.

As deep as her feelings for Clark ran, Chloe's need to find out the truth about things ran deeper. Maybe if they'd become a couple, as she'd hoped, her fascination with him would have taken a different direction. But they hadn't, and now her interest was more inquisitive than anything else. She couldn't help but want to chase down the answers to her many questions about him, even though she suspected that eventually, her pursuit might carry a high price.

CHAPTER 17

I still can't believe you didn't get hurt," Luna said with wonder as she stroked Clark's hair. They were in the living room, having just finished a dinner of fast-food cheeseburgers (that Clark had insisted on paying for; after the pizza incident, he'd sworn not only that he wouldn't steal, but that he wouldn't eat anything that had ever been *near* a garbage can ever again) and slices of birthday cake left over from a celebration at the New-Age store where Luna worked. Meals here were like that, Clark was learning — a mishmash of whatever was cheap or free. At first it was fun to eat junk food all the time, but now he was starting to really miss his mother's cooking.

The nice part was that everyone else was out,

so Clark and Luna had the house to themselves. Since it was a little chilly, Clark had found some broken table legs on the second floor and had given them a quick zap with his heat vision while Luna wasn't looking. Now they sat warming by the fireplace.

"And I can't believe that lie Sean told you about him being with me," Luna said with annoyance. "That makes me so mad."

Not as mad as I am about him throwing a bottle at us, Clark thought, but he saw no point in bringing it up. There had been no sign of Sean and, besides, there was another matter that Clark hadn't been able to push out of his mind.

"Luna . . . there was something else Sean said."

"I can't even imagine," Luna said, rolling her eyes. "Tell me."

"He, um . . . Well, I don't know what he meant by it, but he said you were a witch."

At first Clark thought the look on Luna's face was shock. Then he saw that it was much different and went far deeper than that. And there was something so familiar about that look. . . .

Slowly, Clark realized what it was. It was the same expression he'd worn when Lex had questioned how he hadn't hit Clark with his car. When Lana had expressed her disbelief about how he'd found her after the tornadoes. Whenever anyone had seen him do something that couldn't be explained.

It was the look of someone who had something to hide.

"He . . . he shouldn't have told you that," Luna stammered. "At least . . . not until I did."

"You mean . . . it's *true*?" Clark asked, stunned.

Luna folded her arms protectively in front of herself. "Don't look at me like that," she pleaded. "I'm the same person I was five minutes ago."

Déjà vu, Clark thought. It was almost exactly what he'd said to Pete when he'd told his best friend the truth about himself. He remembered the horrible way Pete had stared at him, like Clark was suddenly a *thing* instead of a *person*. He didn't want to do that to Luna. "I'm sorry," he said. "It's just that — I don't even really know what all this means."

"Well," Luna said, "what does it mean to you?"

Clark thought about it. "I don't know. Aren't witches supposed to be evil green hags with warty noses who make poisoned apples for a living? You don't seem too evil," he said. "Or green." It was the right thing to say; they both laughed, breaking the tension in the room.

Uncrossing her arms, Luna exhaled. "Ever since I can remember, I felt like I was . . . different," she began. "When I was little, I always knew who was calling before anyone answered the phone. I thought animals could mentally talk to me. Like, once, when our dog was really sick, I told my parents that he said he'd swallowed a pair of my dad's rolled-up socks. The whole car ride to the vet's, they were scolding me: 'LuAnne Dobson, animals don't talk. You saw that in *Dr. Doolittle.*' Well, they had to operate on our dog." She paused. "Guess what they found?"

"Your dad's socks," said Clark, though he wasn't sure he believed her. *No, I don't want to believe her,* he thought. *If it's true, if she can sense things about people, she might be able to figure out my secret.* Was it possible? He couldn't help but wonder about it.

"One night, I had a dream that my dad died," Luna continued, looking down and fiddling nervously with her rings. "He was in his car, and then all of a sudden he was flying up and away somewhere. And he was happy." She wiped at her eyes. "A week later, when he was coming home from work, he was hit by a drunk driver."

"I'm so sorry," Clark said softly.

Luna looked up at him. "But it was like he didn't really die, Clark," she said. "I mean, I know he did, physically. But I always felt like he was still with us. And he'd talk to me in my dreams, tell me that he loved us and that he was okay." Clark was silent; he didn't want to say that it sounded like the way any kid would react. He couldn't imagine how insane he'd go if he lost one of his parents.

As if sensing what he'd thought, Luna went on. "But he'd tell me more specific things, too, like where to find a bracelet I'd lost, or that my mom needed to get her heart checked out because she had a murmur. And he was always right.

"Anyway," Luna continued, "I think I drove Mom over the edge when I tried to tell her about this. She'd get really mad, scream at me to stop. She thought I was on drugs or something. So she tore apart my room, and when she found the candles and my tarot cards . . ." Luna shrugged. "She just thought I'd lost it. She started calling psychiatrists."

Clark was shocked. "That's why you ran away," he said.

Luna sighed. "I love my mom, Clark, but she thought I was a freak. Some of my friends did too. Have you ever felt that way?"

"More than you know," Clark said.

"I can't believe that," she said, smiling. "You're so normal, it's like you're from another planet. Your parents must adore you."

"I guess so . . . I mean, I know they do."

"You miss them, don't you," said Luna.

Clark nodded. "And they're probably losing their minds worrying about me, but I don't want to call because they might figure out where I am."

Luna's face suddenly brightened. "There is something we could do — a way to contact them, send them a message without blowing it about where you are."

"E-mail?" Clark asked.

"More like *dream*-mail," Luna said. "That is . . . if you're okay with all of this. With the witch thing. With me."

Clark grinned at her. "For the record, I still don't think you're green enough to qualify as a witch, but I also don't think you're a freak," he said. Luna's face was full of relief and gratitude, the same feelings Clark had when Pete started treating him like his best friend again.

She pushed herself closer to Clark until their knees touched, and took his hands. "Okay, close your eyes," she instructed. "And pick just one of your parents, like your mom. It'll get too blurry if you try to do both." Clark didn't know what she meant, but he closed his eyes and thought of his mother.

"Now really concentrate on her. Think of where she'd probably be right now. Try to 'find' her," Luna said, her voice becoming a soft whisper.

A vision of Clark's house came into his mind.

It was so real it seemed like he was actually there. He searched around the living room, looked up the stairs, and then peeked into his parents' room. There they were, asleep. His father was a little shadowy, but the vision of his mother was clear enough for Clark to see the troubled look on her face as she slept. Her eyes were puffy from crying.

Luna's voice sounded like it was coming from far away now, even though she was still holding his hands. "Now talk to her — quietly, so you don't wake her up." Vaguely, Clark was aware that Luna must be seeing, or at least sensing, what he saw, which was kind of amazing. But he was too preoccupied by the strong sensation of being home to think much about that.

I'm okay, Mom. Don't worry about me — everything's fine. I love you and Dad, and I'll be home soon. Please don't cry . . .

"Clark?" Was it his mother calling him, or was it Luna? Clark wasn't sure, but he suddenly felt like he was at the end of a giant bungee cord that had been snapped back. There was a *whoosh*, and he was flying over the farm, over the road, over the Metropolis skyline, over the Tribe's house, and then *bam!* His eyes popped open and he was back in the living room.

"What . . ." Clark shook his head. "Wow! What happened?"

"I think it worked," Luna said with a grin, unable to contain her excitement. "And I think you woke your mom."

❧ ❧ ❧ ❧

Later that night, Clark couldn't sleep. At first it was because he kept thinking about the strange experience Luna had led him through. His house, his parents — all of it had been so vivid, like he'd really been there. He had no idea how she'd done it, or if she'd even done anything at all.

But then he just felt a giant wave of homesickness that he couldn't find a way to fight. If he closed his eyes, he saw his mother's tear-stained face; if he opened them, he saw this cold, filthy room with its broken windows and cracked walls.

And there was something new that he hadn't noticed before: the scratchy sound of rats as they scurried across the floors and in the spaces between the walls. There was only one comfort in this place.

Reaching over gently so he wouldn't wake her, he held Luna's hand.

CHAPTER 18

Ahhh, there's my speeding bullet."

"'Morning, Mr. Grimes," Clark said as he walked into Mercury Messengers. "Got something for me?"

"I got a lot for you, kid," Mr. Grimes mumbled through his chomped-on cigar. "Starting today, all the rush jobs go to you. I don't know how you've been delivering these packages so fast, but keep it up and you'll have a decent check waiting for you at the end of the week." Clark's smile was huge; that was exactly what he'd come to Metropolis for. *I'll send the money to Mom and Dad, keep just a little for food and emergencies,* he thought happily.

"Okay, kid," said Mr. Grimes as he ripped a slip

of paper off a pad. "Here's your first job of the day. There's a pickup at this address, then take it to the newsroom at the *Daily Planet*. Call me when you're done and I'll have more for you. If only the rest of you bums were as fast as this kid with no bike!" he yelled at the other messengers as he handed over the address.

Clark sprinted out of the messenger center, motivated more at that moment by embarrassment than money.

🦀 🦀 🦀 🦀

It was harder to run as fast as he could in Metropolis than it was in Smallville. There, Clark could speed along the roads and there wouldn't be anyone around to see him. Here, there were people and cars and bikes and dogs and everything in the way. Not wanting to have another accident like he had with his father's tractor, he found it easier to run in alleyways and even above the streets, where he could jump the short distance between rooftops.

In this way, it took him only a few minutes to get from the messenger center to an apartment building, pick up the package to be delivered, and run to the *Daily Planet*, which was right next door to the LuthorCorp building. Clark had remembered that from a previous trip to Metropolis, so he was careful not to linger too long outside. *It'd be just my luck that Lex would be coming to work right about now,* he thought.

Once inside the newspaper building, though, Clark had to stop and admire the giant globe, with the words DAILY PLANET on it, revolving in the middle of the floor. It was really cool, and after showing his messenger ID to the guard at the door, Clark wandered around the circumference of the globe before he remembered why he was there.

"May I help you?" asked the receptionist on the newsroom floor, high up in the building.

"Yes, I have a package for a . . . Samuel Brown," Clark read off the label.

"Hmmm, Samuel Brown," said the receptionist. "Oh, yes, he's the new reporter. Through this door, all the way to the end, last cubicle on your right."

When he opened the glass door, Clark couldn't believe the hum of activity in the newsroom. It was a huge open floor of cubicles with people walking purposefully all over the office. The clacking of keyboards was constant, there was an electronic news zipper near the top of the far wall, and people in corner offices had TVs tuned to news stations around the country. Another wall was full of clocks with times for London, Paris, Munich, Singapore. . . . Clark walked slowly down an aisle, trying to take it all in.

At the far end of the floor, at a tiny work-station, was a guy of about Lex's age, twenty-four or twenty-five, who had a phone jammed to his ear and was trying to take down notes at a mile a minute. He didn't notice Clark standing there, and Clark took the time to look around the newsroom floor again.

"You say those buildings are landmarks, but they're going ahead with the plans for the chemical plant anyway?" Samuel Brown was saying into the phone. "But they can't do that unless — bribery? Who? Come on, you've got to tell me where this came from or I can't run the story. If I print any of this without naming a source, I won't be able to write for a high school newspaper after LuthorCorp's lawyers get through with me!"

At the mention of LuthorCorp, Clark spun around, which made Samuel notice him for the first time. "I've got to go. Call me later when you get something more solid," he said, hanging up the phone. "What can I do for you?"

"Package for you," Clark said, handing him the envelope. He wanted to ask why Mr. Brown had been talking about Lex's father's business, but he knew it was none of his own.

"Thanks, kid," said Samuel. He watched as Clark took a lingering look at the newsroom. "Pretty cool, isn't it?"

"It's . . . amazing," Clark said. "Is it always like this? This crazy, this exciting?"

Samuel nodded. "And this is a slow news day," he said. "But maybe it'll pick up. I'm new here, and I'm looking for my first big story. Who knows," he said, looking at his heavily scribbled-on notepad, "maybe I've got one."

Clark was trying to think of a way to ask what the story was about and how it involved Lex, but just then his walkie-talkie squawked to life with Mr. Grimes's voice. "Hey, Fast Kid! Come in!"

"I've got to go," said Clark, dragging himself away. "It was nice to meet you."

"See you around," said Samuel, already dialing his phone.

☙ ☙ ☙ ☙

Clark did one more spin around the globe in the *Daily Planet*'s lobby before he left the building. He was ecstatic with an idea that had come to him in the elevator on the way down: *I want to work here.*

He took in every detail of the lobby, imagining the day he'd flash his reporter's ID card to the guard at the door, go to a tiny cubicle like Mr. Brown's, and work hard on news stories. Reporting was something that Clark had thought about from time to time when the school guidance counselors grilled him about what he'd choose for his major when he went to college, but seeing that newsroom . . . Clark was grinning with excitement. He'd found what he wanted to do. It felt like falling in love, only *The Daily Planet* wasn't going to say it just wanted to be friends. He couldn't wait to tell Luna.

"Kid! Are you there or *what*?" crackled Mr. Grimes over the walkie-talkie.

"Uh, right here!" Clark said. "Sorry about that — where's my next pickup?"

"Hit the Campbell, Morgan, and Davis Law Firm at Nineteenth and James, and take the envelope to LuthorCorp."

Oh no, Clark thought. What if Lex was there and saw him? "Uh . . . is there anyone else who can take that job, Mr. Grimes?"

"It's a super-rush, kid," Mr. Grimes crackled back. "I need you. And it pays extra if you get it there before noon."

Clark took a second to weigh the risk. "I'm on it," he said.

CHAPTER 19

Clark's excitement over the *Daily Planet* morphed into nervousness as he left the law firm and headed for LuthorCorp, a thick legal envelope under his arm. He was dismayed to see that it was addressed to Lex and Lionel Luthor, which meant they were both here in Metropolis. What if he had to deliver it directly to them? Clark might as well give up on his plan, call his parents himself, and tell them he wouldn't be late for dinner tonight.

But luck was on his side. All deliveries went to a messenger center in the basement, and there was zero chance that Lex would be down there. Relieved, Clark dropped off the envelope and headed back up to the lobby.

Clark had been so worried about being spotted by Lex that he hadn't noticed the flyer taped to a wall by the door at LuthorCorp when he'd come in. He saw it now, though, on his way out. On it was a picture of his own face — the class photo of him from the Smallville High School yearbook, taken last year. He hated that photo, in which he was looking awkwardly to one side, wearing a tie that was too tight and a self-conscious half-smile because Lana was next in line to get her picture taken.

But it got worse. Written below the embarrassing photo in huge block letters was: HAVE YOU SEEN ME? MISSING: CLARK KENT. REWARD, with a phone number and information about him — his age, height, hair and eye color, where he was last seen . . .

Lex must have had these put up all over the city to help Clark's parents find him. Trying not to be noticed, Clark reached up and gently tore the flyer off the wall as he walked out.

☙ ☙ ☙ ☙

There must be more of these around here, Clark thought. Sure enough, there was another one taped to a lamppost outside of LuthorCorp, then another on a bus shelter down the block. As usual in Metropolis, nobody paid any attention to anything around them, so Clark was free to peel his picture off the various structures unnoticed.

Clark was crumpling up the flyers and stuffing them in his messenger bag as he walked past an alleyway around the corner from the LuthorCorp building. He glanced down the alley to see if there were any flyers there, and he thought he saw another familiar face — not his own, but Sean's.

He hadn't been spotted, so Clark just kept walking. But once he was behind the opposite wall, he leaned around the brick wall to look again. It was definitely Sean — Clark recognized his sharp blue eyes under his construction helmet — and he was standing with a small, nervous-looking guy in a suit.

There was so much traffic going past that Clark

couldn't hear exactly what they were saying. Random words floated on the air in his direction.

"... Suspicious ..." said the man in the suit.

Sean waved his hand dismissively. "Don't you worry about ... Just ..."

"How will you ... ?"

Clark cursed the noisy traffic. He couldn't figure out what was going on, but if Sean was involved, it couldn't be good.

Then Sean held out his hand, making a quick *gimme* gesture with his fingers. The man looked around, then handed Sean a fat envelope. Clark was shocked by the amount of cash that Sean began counting. Then the man nodded at Sean and began walking down the other direction in the alley, toward the LuthorCorp building. And Sean began heading toward Clark.

Quickly, Clark hid in the doorway of a diner a few doors up and watched from within as Sean went past. Then, waiting until he was a safe distance away, Clark followed him down into a subway station.

CHAPTER 20

Mr. Luthor?" One of the many junior assistants that fluttered around LuthorCorp poked his head into the giant conference room, where Lex sat alone. "The package you were waiting for just arrived." He handed it to Lex, who looked surprised. "That was fast," he said before dismissing the assistant.

He had only a moment to leaf through the thick file before he heard the door open again.

"Lex," Lionel Luthor said, "is that what I think it is?"

"Good morning to you too, Dad," Lex grimaced. He couldn't wait for this chemical plant deal to be over. Lionel had come to Smallville to talk about the plans, and then he'd come with

Lex to Metropolis to make sure they went through without a hitch. Anyone who didn't know the two would think that father and son were incredibly close, the way Lionel was following Lex's every move on this project. *Funny*, Lex thought, *that he spent most of his life trying to distance himself from me, and now I'd like nothing better than to be far away from him.*

"Well, son," Lionel said as his hand searched for a chair, "what do our lawyers have to say about the property in downtown Metropolis?"

"The buildings qualify as historical landmarks," Lex stated flatly. Lionel's expression was stony. "That means no chemical plant," Lex said, trying to make sure his father understood him. "Those buildings have to be turned over to the city for restoration. They can't be demolished."

His father's expression didn't show a hint of what he was thinking. "Have you told anyone but me about this?" Lionel asked.

"No . . . ," Lex answered, wondering what his father was up to. "I think the lawyers spoke to Hal Trumble, but that's it."

"Our demolition and construction team has no idea, then."

"Yes, but *we* know," Lex said. "We can't just go ahead with the demolition . . ."

"Why not?" Lionel demanded. "We already own the property those buildings are standing on. If this report had come a day or two later, most of them would have already met with the wrecking ball!"

"But it didn't," Lex insisted. "It's here now. We can't go ahead with the plans for the plant. We have to find another location."

Lionel smiled in a way that chilled Lex's blood; he wasn't completely immune to his father's predatory instincts. "That real estate was too expensive for me to give it up so easily, Lex. And I hear those buildings are very old, unstable. I'm not at all sure they can be refurbished."

"Of course they can, that's not —"

"Some of the members of the city planning committee happen to agree with me on that point, Lex," Lionel said matter-of-factly.

"You've got them in your pocket," Lex said,

with near-admiration in his voice. "You know, I came here looking for corruption and bribes in the company, but I had no idea it reached this high up."

Lionel looked surprised. "I'll admit to no such thing," he said. "I have no control over what other people will do in the name of progress, especially when they feel that they are under intense pressure to keep their jobs. But I'll tell you one thing, Lex," Lionel said, rising to his full height. "It continues to amaze me how much you like to pretend to be innocent about how business works. And it's commendable the way you want everything to have a happy ending.

"But," Lionel said with an edge, "you need to stop trying to play the part of the hero, son. That's for other people, like your friend Clark Kent. It's not part of your destiny. And it never will be."

Lex tried not to flinch when Lionel reached out to pat his son's cheek in a mock-affectionate gesture. Lex had vowed long ago to do everything in his power to keep from becoming like his father, but part of him knew with chilling certainty that what Lionel said was true.

❧ ❧ ❧ ❧

"Sean!" Clark called out. He was walking down the subway platform toward the leader of the Tribe.

Just a few feet ahead, near the beginning of the tunnel that led to the next train station, Clark watched Sean whirl around suddenly. When he saw Clark, his expression went from surprised to angry, but only for a second. "Clark," he said innocently. "What's up, man? What are you doing here?"

"Working," said Clark. "What are *you* doing here?"

"Same," Sean said.

"Your job seems to pay a lot better than mine," Clark said.

"I don't know what you mean," Sean said, slowly walking around Clark so that he was nearer to the exit. Clark was prepared to grab him at a second's notice, as soon as they finished playing this little game.

"I saw you with that guy, with all that money," Clark insisted. "What was that about?"

Caught, Sean dropped all pretense of being pleasant. "Stay out of it, Clark, if you know what's good for you."

"Or what — you'll throw another bottle at me?" The sound of an approaching train rumbled in the throat of the tunnel.

"You don't seem to be able to take a hint very well," Sean said, leaning toward Clark so he could be heard above the roar of the oncoming train. "Maybe I shouldn't be so subtle."

Suddenly, he pushed Clark as hard as he could. Clark didn't even hit the tracks before the train ran into him full force, sending him into the darkness of the tunnel. Clark heard a high-pitched shriek. Whether it was the train's brakes or the screams of the people on the platform, he couldn't tell.

CHAPTER 21

Blackness everywhere.

Clark blinked a few times and realized that he wasn't unconscious, he was just lying in a dark tunnel. In fact, he wasn't hurt at all, but he'd never been hit by a train before, and the impact had knocked him senseless for a moment. He shook his head clear and slowly rose to his feet.

In front of him was the train with a Clark-sized dent in it. *Looks like something out of a cartoon*, he thought disjointedly. Behind him was the tunnel leading to the next station. He heard a commotion on the platform around the train. People were shouting, "I saw him! He pushed that guy on the tracks and ran away!" "Oh my God, is he dead?" "Somebody back the train up!" "Call the police!"

Clark couldn't go back up that way, even if the train wasn't blocking him — there would be too many questions. It would be better to just disappear altogether. He took a last head-clearing breath and sped through the tunnel to the next station.

On that platform, people were looking to see if the train was coming when Clark climbed up the side stairs leading out of the tunnel. The sight of Clark, filthy from his fall and emerging from the darkness, made them stare even more.

"Uh . . . just doing some track work," he said lamely to the people nearest to him. "Train's probably going to be delayed for a while. Sorry . . ." Then he ran up the stairs and out of the station.

☙ ☙ ☙ ☙

At night, the Tribe's house was dark, but not completely. Light from the streetlamps outside shone in through the slats that boarded up the broken windows. *The city's equivalent of stars*, Clark thought to himself.

He looked over at Luna, who was also still awake. "Hey," Clark whispered, "what's the matter?"

"I'm worried about Sean. Not worried that something's happened to him," she added quickly. "But . . . I don't know. I feel like he's up to something."

Clark hadn't told her about seeing Sean with the man in the alleyway because he didn't know how to explain the part about the train. Sean hadn't been at the house when Clark got back, so he had decided to keep quiet about the whole incident for now. "What is it, then?" he asked.

"I've been having dreams about this house," Luna said. "And the other buildings in the neighborhood, and money, and Sean. I don't know what it all means, but I've got a feeling Sean's up to something. And whatever it is, if he gets busted . . . the cops will figure out we're here and we'll all be on the next bus home."

Clark thought of everything and everyone he missed in Smallville. "Would that be so bad?"

There was a rustling of a sleeping bag nearby as

someone turned over. Clark and Luna waited until it was quiet again, then they inched closer together so they wouldn't be heard.

"I don't know," Luna whispered. "But it would be sad because the Tribe wouldn't be a family anymore. And we wouldn't be together anymore."

Clark didn't know what to say. Part of him very much wanted to go home, but part of him wanted to stay here in this awful place with Luna forever. He watched her face, illuminated by the slats of light from outside. She was looking down, absently stroking his fingers. Suddenly, he found himself leaning over to kiss her.

Clark was surprised at himself. He wasn't used to being impulsive, or to being able to show his affection for someone. For the longest time he'd had to keep his feelings for Lana in check, but with Luna, everything was different. She wasn't afraid to show her true feelings, and Clark felt like he didn't have to hide himself from her. At least, *this* part of himself.

"What was that for?" she said, smiling.

Clark felt slightly self-conscious. "Because . . . I think you're beautiful."

Luna smiled in a way that meant she was probably blushing, though in the dark, it was hard to tell. "Yeah, right," she said. "I think a pair of glasses is in your future."

Again, someone tossed restlessly. Clark mouthed *shhhh* and put his fingers to Luna's lips. Slowly, with the lightest touch, he traced the outline of her mouth, then stroked her cheek. He leaned over and kissed her forehead, her eyelids, the tip of her nose and her lips. *Home*, he realized, was in this moment, and he wanted it to last forever.

CHAPTER 22

The next morning, Clark almost bolted from his sleeping bag before he realized it was Saturday and he didn't have to go to work. He sank back in, sleepily wondering what time it was. Probably early, but it was impossible to tell from looking out the window. It was one of those dark fall days that was the same color gray in the morning as it was at night.

He looked around. Luna wasn't there, but Aubrey, Mag, and Skunk were still curled up tightly in their sleeping bags. Clark dressed quickly. It was chilly in the room, and the place was going to be brutal in the wintertime with only the fireplace to keep them warm.

He'd just pulled on a sweater when he stepped

out onto the roof, and what he saw made him stop in the doorway. Luna was in her usual spot facing the sunrise, which on this day was just a brighter gray spot in the clouds. But this morning, she was standing in the middle of a space marked by four white candles. In a little pile in the center of the circle were things Clark recognized as belonging to the other members of the Tribe — one of Skunk's studded cuffs, Mag's teddy bear, Aubrey's Discman, and one of his own blue T-shirts.

Luna began to turn clockwise, her arm outstretched, her eyes closed. "I cast this circle for the good of all and harm to none — Clark," she said, opening her eyes.

"Hey," he said tentatively. "What are you doing?"

She hesitated, weighing a decision in her mind. "Come here," she beckoned. "Wait." With her finger she cut the air around Clark in the shape of a doorway. "Now come in."

Clark had to smile as he stepped next to her. "Okay, what was that?"

"I had to cut a doorway in the circle," she said, tracing her finger in the opposite direction.

"But there's nothing there."

"Nothing you can see," she said. "And to answer your question, I'm casting a spell of protection over all of us — that's why this stuff is here," she said, indicating the pile. "I needed something from everyone that had her or his essence on it. Of course, it's better when you can have the actual person with you," she said, taking his hand. "I just didn't want to wake everybody up and freak them out."

Clark frowned. "Freak them out about what? Did you have a dream or something?"

"No," Luna answered. "I got this." She held up a tarot card marked "The Tower." On it was a drawing of a building being struck by lightning. The building was on fire, and people were falling out of the windows.

"That doesn't look like good news," Clark said.

"It's not. Usually it just means change is coming, but it can also mean danger. Between that and the funny feelings I've been having, I thought I should cast a spell to keep us safe."

Clark looked deeply into Luna's eyes. His heart reached for her, but his mind held back. "Luna, do you really believe in spells, in magic?" He paused. "That you're a witch?"

"I do, Clark," said Luna, her face serious. "It's my faith. It's who and what I am. You know I'd never do anything to hurt you or anyone else — that's not what witches do. This is just . . . I don't know if you've ever done something that you thought was impossible, because you wanted to help another person, but that's what this is about. We might be in trouble, and this is something that I can do to help. I know it seems strange to you. Maybe *I* seem strange to you. And . . . it's okay if you don't understand. If you don't want to be here," she whispered.

Clark wrapped his arms around her. "I do understand," he said, "and I want to stay." Luna gave him a squeeze and smiled.

"So . . . what do I do?" asked Clark.

"Just stay in the middle for now," she said.

He watched as she walked around the circle twice. On the third time, she stopped at each candle and asked the elements of air, fire, water, and earth to bless the circle. Then Luna faced east and said, in a prayerful tone:

Blessed Mother and Father, I invoke thee;
I ask your protection for my friends and me.
Please take us in your loving arms;
Watch over us, keep us from harm.

She leaned down and shook a bunch of sweet-smelling herbs around the Tribe members' belongings and around where she and Clark stood, then placed a few crystals around that. She finished by drawing a white chalk circle around herself, Clark, and the little pile.

Clark felt the tingle of goosebumps rising on his skin, but it wasn't from the chill air. Even though the sky was still bleak and he could hear wind blowing, he suddenly felt warm and cozy, like someone had just wrapped a soft blanket around him. *Strange*, he thought.

"Ready?" Luna asked. She took his hands and began to spin, slowly at first, and then faster, their arms stretching taut, fingers clasping each other's hands tightly.

"What are we doing?" Clark said, watching everything behind Luna spin in a blur.

"Raising energy!" Luna was laughing and

panting with the effort, her hair whipping around behind her. "Keep going, keep going, keep going — okay, *now*!"

She stopped abruptly and threw her arms and Clark's upward, then sank to her knees with her arms crossed over her heart and her eyes closed. Clark sat down, breathing hard. *That was fun, but what* . . .

His senses prickled, but not in warning. He looked at Luna, then refocused his eyes so he could see in X-ray vision. Luna turned into a kneeling skeleton whose breath was slowing down. The candles and the pile in the center of the circle looked like the negative of a photo, black to white and white to black. And there was something else.

At first Clark thought his eyes were playing tricks on him, but he blinked a few times and he could still see it: a field of blue, swirling around them and reaching up toward the sky. *What is that?* Clark wondered. *Energy?* He had never been able to see energy before, not in all the times since he'd learned how to use his special sight. Gradually, the blue field swirled upward and disappeared.

"What is it?" Luna had been watching him. "Did you see something?"

"Yeah," Clark said, too amazed to pretend he hadn't.

"Cool" was all that Luna said. "We're done. I just have to open the circle."

Clark was still puzzling over what he'd seen as Luna walked counterclockwise this time, thanking the elements and stopping as she faced east. "This circle is open, but never broken," she said. She knocked on the tar rooftop three times.

"Now what?" asked Clark.

Luna shrugged, looking wary. "We wait. And watch. And," she managed a smile, "we go get some breakfast."

☙ ☙ ☙ ☙

The rest of the day passed with no threat on the horizon. Clark celebrated his first paycheck as a messenger by treating Luna to breakfast, even though she told him he'd never be able to send money home if he went around treating

157

people all the time. He pointed out that pancakes weren't exactly going to break the bank, and she had to agree.

After breakfast, the sun peeked out through the clouds, making it a nicer day than they'd expected, so they walked to Metropolis Park. They sat under a tree in comfortable silence for a while, Luna's head resting on Clark's shoulder, Clark weaving a lock of her hair through his fingers. For now, any thoughts of Sean and what he might be up to were far from his mind.

When the sky turned dark blue with the approaching night, Clark suggested that they gather up fallen branches for the fireplace. "Wow, look at that one," Luna said, pointing to a branch almost as big as the tree it had fallen from. "Too bad we don't have a chainsaw to break that up. That'd keep us warm forever."

Clark waited until she wandered off a little way, then braced one foot against the huge limb and began cracking it into smaller pieces. He caught up with her, an innocent look on his face and three large logs under his arm.

"Hey! How did you —"

Clark shook his head. "Uh-uh, that's a farm secret. I can't share things like that with city people, or you'll just go around breaking up your own logs and you won't need me anymore."

Luna squeezed his hand. "That's not going to happen," she said. Slowly they headed downtown, back home. It was the first time Clark had thought of the cold, abandoned building as his home. And it was, for now.

As he walked with Luna, Clark wondered if she missed her friends from home as much as he missed his. Maybe Skunk had been her best friend in Miami, so she was lucky to have him here. But did she have someone that meant to her what Lana had meant to Clark? Someone who was so close, yet somehow always out of reach? Someone who it hurt to love?

Clark ached for his family and friends, but another part of his heart felt lighter than he could ever remember. All his life he'd felt apart from everyone else, alone, because he could do things that other people couldn't do. Luna had said she'd felt different too, and she was — so different from anyone Clark had ever known.

He didn't know if she really had some sort of power, despite the blue energy thing he'd seen in her circle that morning and her prophetic dreams. He didn't know if he even believed in witches or magic. But Clark felt a bond with Luna. He felt that somehow they were on the same level, two of a kind. *And if that isn't magic,* Clark thought, *I don't know what is.*

What —

CHAPTER 23

What —

Clark's eyes flew open. He had been sleeping dreamlessly, and something woke him up with a start.

The answer was right in front of his face, literally: Luna's orange-striped kitten was staring at him with wide blue eyes. She let out a little squeak and batted at his nose, the pads on her tiny paws soft against his skin.

"Hey Rover," he whispered. He looked over at Luna's sleeping bag; it was empty. The living room was dark and quiet but for the deep, even breathing of the rest of the Tribe. Clark reached over to stroke the kitten. "Where's our friend —"

He withdrew his hand. There was something

slick on Rover's fur. He couldn't see what it was in the dark, but he recognized the sharp odor instantly.

Gasoline? Rover squeaked at him again insistently, like she was trying to tell him something.

A cold feeling set roots in Clark's stomach and spread. He was suddenly awake and alert. Slowly but deliberately, he got out of his sleeping bag and pulled on his clothes. Then he tiptoed out of the room and down the stairs.

❧ ❧ ❧ ❧

He was just reaching the second floor when he heard a sound like the splatter of liquid, then another. He saw a shadow move against a wall of the second-floor living room and disappear. Clark narrowed his eyes as he tried to look into the room with his X-ray vision, but something was wrong — he couldn't see through the walls. There was only one thing that could block his X-ray vision, and that was lead. Looking around, he realized that the building was so old that the paint, years and layers of it, must have been lead-based.

Quietly, he stepped inside the room.

Slits of light came in from the street through the cracked windows, leaving slices of illumination along the walls. The rest was all shadow, with mysterious masses that Clark knew were piles of old, broken furniture but which, in the dark, made malevolent shapes. He took another step and felt the floor become slick under his shoe. More gasoline.

Instinctively, Clark looked up just in time to see a large, shiny object sailing toward his head. He went into super-speed mode and, in a split second, saw that it was a big metal can as he swung his arm to knock it away. It flew to the other side of the room, spraying everything with gasoline.

"How the hell are you still alive?" Sean growled. "That train should've knocked you right back to wherever you came from!"

Clark could see Sean now, but he wasn't that easy to get to. The piles of old furniture formed a tight maze, and even as Clark shoved the ancient couches, tables, and broken chairs aside, Sean slid through, under, and around them.

"Sean," Clark demanded, "what are you doing?!"

A bitter laugh came from behind an old bureau. "Y'know, everything was fine around here until you showed up, Clark. You're a pretty nosy guy. But since you asked . . . I'm making a living."

Clark pushed another stack of dead furniture aside. There wasn't much space to move around — for all his strength, things were packed so tightly in the room that there was hardly anything he could do to get to Sean, who kept dodging him. "What do you mean, making a living? What's with the gasoline? Sean!"

Again, that sickening laugh. "This old house isn't worth a fraction of the ground it's sitting on, and that guy you saw me with yesterday paid a lot of money to see some fireworks tonight. So I'm having a little building barbecue, Clark. And you're invited." Clark stopped for a second, realizing with horror what Sean planned to do.

"It's too bad you saw me in the alleyway, Clark. I was going to get everybody out first, but you probably went and told them about what happened," Sean said. "And I can't let anybody find out about this. So . . ." There was a small scratching sound, *tchk*, and then a little glow.

"*No!*" Clark shouted.

He frantically began tossing chairs, tables, and bureaus over his shoulders in an effort to get to Sean. He vaguely heard them crashing to the floor behind him. When there were so many that he couldn't push past them, he smashed them to splinters with his fist.

But it was too late. Even as he plowed toward Sean, Clark watched helplessly as a lit book of matches sailed in an arc to the other end of the room. It had barely touched the floor when — *whoosh* — the room turned bright orange with flames that rushed up to the ceiling, devouring the ancient curtains, feeding on the trash in the room.

"So what does a wanna-be hero like you do now?" Sean sneered over the roar of the fire. "My guess, you're going to try to save the Tribe." The room was suddenly so bright that Clark could clearly see Sean's evil grin. "Better hurry. I hear witches burn especially well."

CHAPTER 24

In the split second before Sean turned and ran to climb out the back window, Clark wanted to pounce on him before he got away. But there was no time — he had to wake the Tribe, get them out.

Clark pushed his way through the burning furniture, never feeling the heat of the flames that jumped hungrily at his clothes. In a flash, he was on the third floor shouting, "Wake up! Everybody, get up! *Fire!*"

Aubrey, Mag, and Skunk jumped up out of their sleeping bags as though they'd been hit with cold water. "Clark!" Mag screamed, pointing at his jeans. Clark hadn't realized that one of his pant legs was on fire. He quickly swatted it out and led them into the hall, first Mag, then Aubrey, and, a second or two later, Skunk.

In just the short time it had taken to rouse everyone, the building had become an inferno. Black smoke choked the hallway, making it almost impossible to see or breathe. A column of flame shot straight up from the second floor, threatening to ignite the stairs to the third. Clark, the only one not coughing and covering his face with a T-shirt, leaned over the banister. The fire was coming from the bottom of the staircase on the floor below, but if he lowered people down to the part of the stairs where the fire hadn't yet reached, they could still get out.

He ripped the old banister out of the floor and threw it aside. Then he leaned down to Mag. "Take my hand and hang on tight," he shouted. "I'm going to lower you down!" Mag looked like she was going to protest for a moment, then thought better of it and nodded at Clark. She clasped his arm in a death grip and threw her legs over the side of the floor. Lying on his chest, Clark easily lowered her down as far he could, then let go and plopped her gently down to the other side of the second floor, which was just far enough away from the fire. She looked up, waiting for Aubrey.

"Mag, get out!" Aubrey screamed. "I'll be right behind you!"

It took only another few seconds to lower Aubrey down, and then it was Skunk's turn. Clark had to smile for a moment when he saw Skunk slip Rover into the inside pocket of his denim jacket. The kitten squeaked madly, her tiny eyes wild with fear.

"Dude," Skunk coughed, "you gotta find Luna —"

"I will," Clark vowed. "I won't leave without her. Now *go!*"

🦀 🦀 🦀 🦀

Clark sped up the stairs. He stopped on the fourth floor, tried to use his X-ray vision to see if Luna was there, and was again prevented by the lead in the paint. He didn't want to waste precious seconds searching for her, but he had to make sure. He sped through the floor. Nothing. She had to be on the roof.

The heat was intense as it rose toward the top of the building. Clark tore up the stairs, unaware that his hair was smoking.

In his panic, Clark flung the roof door open so hard that it slammed shut behind him. He gasped with relief: there was Luna, wrapped in her teddy bear coat, her cards in front of her, a white candle long burned out.

Clark shook her shoulders. "Luna! Luna, wake up!" As her eyes opened, she smiled.

"Hey. I must have fallen asleep . . ."

"Luna, we've got to get out of here," Clark said. "The building's on fire."

In a flash, Luna's smile was gone, but she stayed calm as Clark pulled her to her feet and they ran for the stairs. He reached to open the metal door, but Luna stopped him. "Wait," she said. "Feel it for heat."

Clark was so used to being almost indestructible that he sometimes forgot about normal precautions. He put his palm on the door and drew it away. "It's hot," he said. "The fire must be in the stairway already."

"Fire escape!" Luna said. They ran to the rear of the building, but even before they got there, Clark could see the orange glow coming from the lower floors. They looked over the ledge and saw the flames shooting up from the windows below, right through the grating of the fire escape. They quickly moved back.

"Clark," Luna gasped, the first edge of panic creeping into her voice, "what are we going to do?"

CHAPTER 25

The tar under Clark's feet was melting, and he could see flames beyond the far edge. Soon, the roof would collapse right under them, sending him and Luna into the hell below. He looked around desperately, but he saw only two ways out: go through the fire, or jump.

He wasn't afraid for himself. He could walk right through fire and his biggest worry would be whether his clothes burned off his body. He could jump from the top of a building four times higher than this one and land on the ground on his feet.

But there was no way to take Luna through the flames — he wouldn't be able to shield her. They'd catch fire in a minute.

That meant there was really only one way out.

Clark led Luna to the side of the building and looked down. There were no windows, so no flames leapt out. There was also no fire escape. Five stories below was a bunch of old cardboard boxes and junk that had been dumped in the yard.

If I make sure I land on my back, she won't get hurt.

But Luna, sensing his plan, shook her head and backed away. "Clark . . . we can't jump! It's too high! We'll be killed, or —"

"We have to," Clark insisted, holding her hand tightly to keep her from running away. "It's our only chance. Look," he said soothingly, "we'll land right on those boxes. We'll be just like stunt men in the movies." He managed a weak grin, hoping that he was convincing her.

She swallowed hard, trembling. "You think?"

Just then, there was a loud explosion from one of the floors below, followed by shattering glass. There were screams from the street, the Tribe calling out to them. A column of flame roared up the front of the building, and the tar covering that end of the roof began to bubble. The fire was right underneath them.

"Luna —" Clark urged.

"I know, it's the only way," she gasped. "Just give me a second." Clark thought she was trying to summon up enough courage to jump, but instead she took both his hands and interlaced her fingers with his. Then she closed her eyes and whispered something intently. With all the commotion around them, Clark couldn't hear what she was saying, but then she opened her eyes.

"Ready?" Clark asked. Luna nodded.

Balancing carefully, Clark stepped up on the ledge. He pulled Luna up in front of him and wrapped his arms tightly around her. Like a diver about to plunge backward off a board, he steadied himself, trying to gauge how far he'd have to jump to land just right. All around them, thick black smoke began to swirl while intense heat rose from the building. The door to the roof blew open and fire roared out like an animal looking for prey.

It's now or never.

Clark leaned close to Luna's ear. "Trust me," he whispered. Luna nodded again and pulled his arms tighter against her.

He held his breath as they jumped backward into the darkness.

CHAPTER 26

Clark knew he wouldn't get hurt when he hit the ground, but he still squeezed his eyes shut and prayed. *Please don't let her get hurt. Please let me land right so that she doesn't get hurt. Please . . .*

Something was wrong. Not "wrong," but it felt like they were suspended in the air. It wasn't what Clark usually felt when he went into super-speed, which he hadn't done. It felt more like they were . . . floating.

Clark dared to open his eyes. He saw the black field of the night sky, but this time it was punctuated by bright stars — the first ones he'd seen since he'd gotten to Metropolis. They were beautiful . . . and then they were blotted out by black smoke.

Suddenly, everything rushed away, and he heard the crunch of cardboard boxes giving way underneath him, then the crack of wood splintering. He gripped Luna's waist with one arm and protected her face with his free hand. Finally, they came to a stop, covered in debris.

Luna wasn't moving. *Oh no*, Clark thought, horrified. Light began to come through over his head, and Clark heard a high-pitched wail in the distance. A second later, he saw that the light was a streetlamp and realized the wail was the sirens of fire engines. Skunk, Aubrey, and Mag were pulling cardboard, chunks of wood, and other garbage away to free them.

"Luna!" Skunk cried. "Clark! Are you guys okay?"

Slowly, Luna's eyes opened, and she looked at Clark, who smiled in relief. Then she hugged him as tightly as she had when they were falling and began to sob.

CHAPTER 27

"You two wait here, and don't go anywhere, okay?" the police officer said. "Child Services will be around soon."

Clark and Luna sat on a bench in the station house of the Metropolis police, Twenty-third Precinct. Even guys being led away in handcuffs stared at the two teenagers whose faces were streaked with soot, their clothes torn and singed, their hands clasped together tightly.

After the fire engines, ambulances had come, but no one was really hurt. Since it was obvious that the kids were runaways who'd been hiding in the building, they'd all been taken to the police station.

Clark looked over at Mag and Aubrey, who

were sitting across the room. "Hey," he asked Luna, "where's Skunk?"

"He took off," she answered. "He made sure we were okay, and I saw him run. He knew what was coming next." Clark looked at her. "We're going home," she explained.

Just then, Clark caught sight of a familiar figure striding through the police station. "Lex!"

"Clark," Lex said, gripping Clark's shoulder with surprising force. "Where have you *been?* You had us all really worried!" His expression was even more serious than usual.

"I'm sorry — I didn't mean to make anybody crazy," Clark said. "I just wanted to . . . well, it's a long story."

"You'll have plenty of time to tell me about it back at my place. We'll stay there tonight and head home tomorrow. Do you want me to call your parents?"

"I already did," Clark said sheepishly. "They were relieved at first, but then they sounded pretty mad."

Lex smiled. "How long are you grounded for?"

"I think they said something about *life*, but I'm not sure," Clark said with a sigh.

The police officer walked up to them. "And you are . . . ?" he asked, looking at Lex.

"His legal guardian in the absence of his parents," Lex said, brandishing a bunch of official-looking papers. The officer examined them.

"Looks okay to me. But just him, not the others." He turned to Luna. "Someone from Child Services is here. You go with her, and don't give her any trouble." Clark saw a kind-looking woman talking to Mag and Aubrey, and Luna slowly stood up.

"Wait," Clark said, "isn't there some way she can come with us?" He looked at Lex pleadingly.

"Not legally," the officer said.

"It's okay, Clark," Luna said, hugging him. "I'll be fine. I'll have Mag and Aubrey with me, and . . ." She pulled open her coat pocket to expose Rover, curled up in a ball and sleeping peacefully.

As they left, Lex noticed a familiar-looking head of pure white hair. It only took him a second to remember Mag, the waitress from the sushi restaurant. He smiled at her, and this time, she rewarded him with a shy wave.

༒ ༒ ༒ ༒

Lex's apartment in Metropolis was the entire penthouse floor of a luxury high-rise building, and Clark would have been impressed if he hadn't been so exhausted. It was nearly morning by the time they got there, and all he wanted to see was a bed.

But when Lex opened the door, the first thing Clark saw was Lana. They just stared at each other for a long second, and then Lana ran up to Clark and threw her arms around him. Clark was speechless.

"I'll, um, get you some towels," Lex said, wandering away.

"Clark, what happened to you? Thank goodness you're all right," Lana said into his sooty shirt. She held onto him tightly, not letting go.

They stayed that way for a long time, each lost in their own thoughts, each surprised by what they were feeling.

CHAPTER 28

Flight Two-O-Seven to Miami will begin boarding in ten minutes at Gate Three," said a voice over the loudspeaker.

"Well," said Luna, "I guess that's me."

Clark watched as she hitched her backpack on her shoulder and picked up a small cat carrier with Rover inside. Lex had very generously bought plane tickets for Luna, Mag, and Aubrey to go home, which, they discovered, wasn't going to be the bad experience they'd been dreading after all. Luna's mother was so happy about having her daughter come back that she was already at the Miami Airport, even though Luna wasn't due there for hours. Mag found out she'd been accepted to a special art school she'd applied to before she ran away, so she was actually looking forward to going home. Even better, her parents had volunteered to temporarily foster Aubrey, so they would still be together.

But there were two members of the Tribe who wouldn't be returning home. Sean had quickly been found by the police and was in the Metropolis Jail. He was in a cell right next to Hal Trumble, and each was trying to blame the other for being the mastermind behind the arson plan.

And then there was Skunk, who was still on the run. Clark was sorry he hadn't had the chance to say goodbye to his new friend, or to thank him for having the presence of mind to not only rescue Rover but to throw the Tribe's backpacks out the window before escaping the fire. He'd taken an insane risk by doing that, when every second counted. But now they all still had the precious mementos they'd brought from home, like Clark's picture of himself with his parents.

In a little while, Clark realized, he'd be home with his family and friends. He wasn't sure how he could be so happy about that and, at the same time, be so miserable. In just a few minutes, Luna would be just a memory.

"Wait," he said, taking Luna's hand. "Before you go, I want you to meet my friends." Not far away, Lex and Lana were waiting for Clark by the landing pad where Lex's helicopter was, but Luna held back. "What's wrong?" Clark asked.

"It's not that I don't want to meet them," she said. "And please, thank your friend Lex for the plane ticket. But . . . this is probably the last time we're going to be together. I just want it to be us."

"Don't be silly," Clark said. "We'll e-mail each other, and we'll figure out a way to —"

"Clark, get real." Luna smiled but rolled her eyes. "Miami's a long way from Smallville, and my mom and your folks are probably never going to let us out of their sight again." She looked over in Lana's direction. "So, is that your girlfriend?"

Clark looked over his shoulder. "No," he said. "She's . . . Lana's a friend . . . but she's not my girlfriend."

"Good," Luna said. "Then she can't say anything about this." She pulled Clark close against her and pressed her mouth against his.

For a second, Clark felt totally self-conscious, kissing another girl in front of Lana. But that melted away as he let himself fall into Luna's kiss. For a moment, he had the same feeling as when they'd jumped off the burning roof, like he was floating, suspended in time.

"This is the final boarding call for Flight Two-O-Seven to Miami," said the loudspeaker voice.

Luna slowly pulled away, but Clark held her hand. "Wait — there's something I wanted to ask you. The night of the fire, up on the roof," Clark continued, "before we jumped, you were saying something to yourself . . . what was it?"

In response, Luna interlaced her fingers with Clark's as she had that night. "I said 'Fly, not fall.' I wished that we would just float down, not hit hard. And at first . . . I know it sounds crazy, but when we jumped off, it didn't feel like we were falling at all, did it?"

"It didn't," Clark said, mystified. Had they both just imagined it? Had Luna's magic really worked? Or . . . he didn't dare consider the other possibility.

"You were flying, Clark Kent," Luna said, finishing his thought. "Remember that feeling. It could come in handy in the future." Then she stood up on her tiptoes and kissed him one last time. "See you in your dreams," she whispered.

Clark watched as Luna disappeared into the plane. For a second, he had a strong urge to run after her, but he had to let it go.

 භ භ භ

Slowly, Clark wandered over to Lex and Lana. "Wow," Lex said, "that was some send-off."

"Who was that, Clark?" Lana asked. Clark couldn't exactly figure out the expression on her face, but there was a tone in her voice he had never heard before.

"A friend," he said.

"Looks like a very special friend," Lex said.

Clark wasn't sure what else to say. There was something different about Lex and Lana. He couldn't put his finger on it, but they somehow seemed closer. It was like the two of them had formed some kind of bond in his absence.

"The helicopter's ready," Lex said. "Let's go."

The three of them walked across the tarmac, Lex striding ahead, Clark and Lana behind. "You never told me what you were doing in Metropolis," Clark said.

"Looking for you," Lana stated simply. "I thought you might be in trouble. But it seems like you were doing fine."

Clark was so thrilled that Lana cared about him enough to skip school and leave everything behind to search for him, that he didn't hear the flat tone in her voice. "Then," he said warily, "I guess we're friends again?"

Lana's familiar smile was quick, but it didn't last. "We'll always be friends, Clark. I'm sure of that. Just . . . really good friends."

Clark wasn't sure why, but he felt like he had just taken a step forward with Lana, only to be pushed two giant steps back.

CHAPTER 29

Clark was on his second helping of meat loaf and mashed potatoes when Jonathan asked, "Son, did you eat at *all* while you were away?" He passed a basket of rolls to Clark.

"Mm-hmm." Clark nodded, chewing. He scooped up a roll and mopped up some gravy. "But I really missed Mom's cooking."

"Not as much as we missed *you*," Martha said, hugging him for the hundredth time that day.

"You didn't worry too much about me, did you?" Clark asked. His parents made identical faces as if to say, *Are you kidding?*

"Clark, we know your intentions were good, but please don't do anything like that again," Jonathan said. "After all, we'll find a way to get a new tractor, and Mr. Reynolds will let you take a make-up exam. This was small potatoes — we're always going to have rough times, but the best way for us to deal with them is by sticking together." Clark smiled. Some of the things his father said were pretty old-fashioned, but he felt the love behind the clichés.

"Well, I've never been so worried in my life," said Martha. "But there was this strange dream I had. It was so clear, not like a dream, but more like . . . It felt like you were here, standing over me, telling me that you were okay and not to worry. And then you said, 'Please don't cry.' And I woke up, and the dream was so real that I felt a little better somehow."

Martha looked at her son, his fork frozen in midair. "I know it seems silly, but it was just a dream, sweetie," she said.

🙰 🙰 🙰 🙰

Late at night, Chloe wandered into Lana's room. Even though the lights were out, she could tell that Lana was still awake too. She sat on the edge of Lana's bed, and Lana didn't seem surprised to see her there.

"You haven't said much about Metropolis," Chloe said.

Lana sighed in the darkness and shifted to face Chloe. "There's not much to say. We found Clark, he was fine, we came home. End of story." Lana wasn't ready to talk about the hot streak of jealousy she'd experienced when she saw Clark kiss that girl. Or the feelings she still hadn't found words for when Lex was looking at her the night they had dinner together, the night he'd told her she was beautiful.

Chloe felt bad about being jealous of Lana for going to Metropolis to look for Clark. Lana looked so sad that Chloe wanted to help more than she even wanted to know what happened.

"Lana . . . I'd like to think we're friends. And I just want you to know that you can tell me anything, and it goes no further."

Smiling, Lana reached over and took Chloe's hand. "You *are* my friend, and I have no fear that my secrets will end up in the *Torch*. I just haven't figured any of this out for myself yet, so it's kind of hard to explain."

At that moment, when it seemed like anything could be said, Chloe found herself suddenly blurting out, "Lana, are you in love with Clark?" She had to know.

If Lana was surprised, she didn't show it, and her voice was soft when she answered. "I think . . . I think that's a very good question, Chloe. But maybe it's one that you should be asking yourself."

Three weeks later, a full moon shone through Clark's bedroom window, beams of white light falling across his bed as he slept. The numbers of the digital clock on the nightstand glowed red in the darkness as they soundlessly changed to 12:00 A.M.

"Hey Clark."

Slowly, Clark began to wake up. "What . . ." He tried to say more, but he suddenly felt a warm pressure on his mouth. Strangely, he wasn't alarmed as he sank back into the bed. It felt like . . . someone was kissing him.

A moment later it was over. Clark opened his eyes more fully and looked around. There was just enough light to see that there was no one else in the room.

Had it been a dream, or . . . ? Clark wasn't sure at first, but then he smiled.

"Hey, Luna," he said, looking outside at the moon. It shone brightly on his face as he slowly fell back to sleep.

About the Author

Suzan Colón is the author of *Smallville: Buried Secrets* and *Catwoman: The Life and Times of a Feline Fatale*. She has also written features for numerous magazines, including *Jane, Mademoiselle,* and *Seventeen*. She lives in New York City.